Guardian Angel
The Arrival

By

A. M. Lahrs

Cyndi,
I hope you
enjoy this.

♡,

A. M.
Lahrs

ISBN: 1-4033-3129-4 (e-book)
ISBN: 1-4033-3130-8 (Paperback)

Library of Congress Control Number:
2002093763

This book is printed on acid free paper.

Printed in the United States of America
Bloomington, IN

1stBooks — rev. 10/14/02

To Shawn,
I made this into story form,
I figured it would be
easier to understand.

Chapter 1

"No way! You cannot send me away! This is also my house, and my life, I think I should maybe have some say in it," I yelled.

"You have to leave, I don't want you to, but you have to get the help, help that I can't give you," My mom said crying.

"I'm not leaving! You can't make me go to that prison," I argued with her.

"It isn't a prison, it is a school to help kids like you," My mother exclaimed.

"I'm not going," I said determined not to leave my house.

"Fine, I can't make you do anything. You can stay here," My mom gave in.

"Good, now I am going out with Gena, Brooke, and Joel," I said to my mom.

"You know I don't like you hanging out with that boy," My mom said.

"I know, but do you honestly think I care?"

"I guess you don't, but can you please put some more clothes on? If you go out like that you'll have strange guys picking you up."

"I'm not changing, I always wear things like this. Besides why would I wear something that won't make guys want to pick me up? I want to make the guys go crazy when they can't get me." I hated it when my mother tried to tell me what to do. It's not like she ever acted like a mother to be by taking care of me, so she shouldn't have the right to start to try and act like a mom.

"But you're practically naked. You have that see through, half shirt on, so that you can see your bra, and that skirt is so high up that your ass is hanging out, and would you please eat something!" My mother said, "Honestly honey you look like a striper."

"Mom, I really am uncomfortable with you swearing at me."

"Well then don't put me into the position to. Also you do it to me, so I don't see the difference of it."

"Mother deary, I do. I actually matter; you don't and everything I say to you and call you are true," I said as I walked out the door.

"Candace!" I heard my mother yelling as I was closing the door. Joel was already parked outside with Gena and Brooke.

"Hey Candy Girl!" Joel said as he kissed me. Brooke and Gena were in the back seat of his old, black Convertible.

"Hi Joel, hey Brooke, Gena what's up?" I said.

"Here, have a drink," Joel said handing me a bottle of beer.

"Thanks, but I rather have some pot, happen to get any?" I asked.

"Yeah here, but don't take too many puffs, this is all I got," Joel said as he handed me the smoke from his hand.

"Thank you."

"We're going to Brent's. He is having a party there and he said for us to stop by and have a few drinks and a couple of smokes," Gena said.

"Cool, I haven't seen Brent in a while," I said.

"Don't you mean you haven't *done* Brent in a while?" Brooke said laughing.

"Same difference, seen him, done him; it is all the same to me," I said laughing. When we got to Brent's place there were millions of

3

people there, or at least it seemed that way. Brent's parties are the biggest thing where I lived, if you weren't there you were nothing to this town, or at least you weren't anything to any of the teenagers in this town. And as far as it went, that was the only thing that mattered in a kid's life. In our town we each had our own parts. People knew us by our parties and also how we acted. Joel was known as the lady killer (he was hot), Gena was known as the bitch of our town, Brooke was the party animal, Brent was called hot rod, he had a fast car, he slept with so many girls, and he had the *greatest* parties of all time. Me, well I was known as many things, the girls knew of me as the slut of the town, and the guys, well they knew me as hotty, a tease, and good. I did do some bad things, lets just say Brent and me are quite alike, just the opposite sex. And if you don't get what I mean, get a life.

"Hey girls, hey Joel," Brent greeted us as he put his arm around me.

"Hi Brent," We all greeted him.

"Candy let's go upstairs, we can talk," Brent said.

"Talking is about the last thing you two are going to do!" Joel yelled as we were walking up the stairs.

"Oh be quiet Joel!" I yelled back. The next thing I remembered was being in Joel's car as he was driving me home.

"Did you and Brent have a good time?" Joel asked.

"I think so, hey we probably had better than a good time," I said then asked, "Where is Gena and Brooke?"

"You really are out of it," Joel said.

"What do you mean?"

"I just dropped them off at Gena's brother's house. They knew they would be in for it if they went home high and drunk, so they told me to take them to David's house. Gena said that David wouldn't care if they walked in high as hell and drunk as shit," Joel explained.

"Oh, that's David for ya."

"Yep and you would know that," Joel said giving me the smile that could win any girl's heart, but mine.

"Hey I didn't do anything with David," I defended myself, "Besides he is too old for me."

"What do you mean? He is the same age as Brent, 19 years old," Joel told me.

"Really? Well I thought he was older and Brent was younger," I said. Since I was only fifteen years old, nineteen seemed kind of old when I thought about it. But hey, Brent and I have had fun, or at least I am guessing that we did. After I'm with him I usually don't remember what happened. Actually I know what happened I just didn't remember it too vividly.

"Well, here you go, we're at your house," Joel informed me.

"I know that, I'm not that out of it. Huh? I wonder who that is," I said pointing to a car that was directly parked in front of the house.

"It's probably your mom's new guy. Your mother isn't going to get mad at you for coming home like this, is she?"

"She usually does, but if she has a guy in there, she will just ignore me," I told him.

"Okay, I was just saying you could come home with me, my parents are away, if you want to you are welcome to come, what do you say?" Joel offered. Joel and I have been friends for awhile and we were always staying over at each other's houses, despite the fact that my mother dislikes him and his mother detests me.

"No it is okay, I am really tired and if I come home with you, I don't think I will be sleeping much. We'll end up talking or drinking all night."

"Okay, well I'll be seeing you when I see you. Bye my Candy Girl," Joel said. He came up with that nickname for me when I yelled at him for calling me Candy Cane.

"C-ya Joel," I said and got out of the car. I walked into my house and I didn't see my mom in the living room, so I figured she was upstairs.

"Mom, I'm home," I called and when I received no answer I thought Joel was right, it was a new guy she had. I walked into my room and saw my mom sitting on my bed with two guys in there. I looked next to my bed and saw a suitcase and bag full of things.

"Hi honey," My mom greeted me.

"Hi," I said self-consciously, "You're moving out mom, and with two guys, jeez, not bad," I said.

"I'm not moving out," My mom said.

"Don't tell me these guys are moving in. That's not going to work," I responded.

"They're not, but you're moving to that school I told you about. I'm sorry, but I have to make you go," My mom told me crying. I knew it was coming right after she told me, that they weren't moving in.

"Like hell you are!" I yelled as I was running down the stairs and out the door. I knew those two guys were running behind me; I could hear their feet hitting the ground. I ran to the corner and saw that Joel was still there. "Joel!" I screamed as loud as I could.

"Candy?" He called out from the driver side window. When he saw the two guys chasing me, he got out of his car and ran toward me. "What is going on?"

"I'll explain later, just get these guys away from me," I demanded him gasping for breath.

"Leave her alone!" Joel yelled to the men, "Get in the car Candy," He ordered me. I went running to the other side of the car and when I was about to get in, one of the guys grabbed me by the arm and tied my hands together with a rope he had.

"Let me go!" I yelled struggling to get loose.

"Leave her the hell alone!" Joel yelled. He was trying to get over to me, but the other man had his arms behind his back.

"We are taking her to a school that her mother is paying for, this has nothing to do with you. Either you get in your car now and leave, or I will call the police and say that we have an under age person who is drunk, and has drugs in his car," The man that was holding me threatened. He was very strong and I couldn't even get somewhat loose from his grip.

"I'm not going anywhere without her," Joel answered.

"Fine, I will call the police now," The other man said as he pulled a cell phone out.

"No!" I yelled, "Let him go. This is between you two guys and me; it has nothing to do with him. Joel, please just leave, you don't need to get in trouble with the cops again."

"Are you sure?" He answered.

"Yeah I'm sure."

"Okay, but call me when you get the chance," He ordered.

"Okay, I will, bye Joel," I knew this was probably the last time I'd see Joel in a while. I also didn't expect to be able to call him, but I figured I'd try anyway.

"Bye Candy," He said and then speeded off.

"Are you going to cooperate with us or are we going to have fun chasing you again?" The one man that was holding me asked and when I didn't answer he started walking me to my house. When we got inside my mother had my bags downstairs and she was saying how sorry she was, but I just ignored her.

"Sweetie I am so sorry," She kept saying over and over. Finally I just couldn't stand it I had to say something,

"Just shut the hell up mom, you're not sorry. If you were sorry, you never would have called these guys to come and take me away!"

"We are sorry that we have to take you away being tied up, but we know that if we untie you, you will run off again," The man said and he probably was right. I would run. "By the way, I am Paul, and this is Travis. We are from the Long Ridge High School in Oregon. It is a school where we help troubled teen. We are going to help you."

"Do you honestly think I care who you are, or where you're from? No matter what you tell me I am still not going to want to go, so let's just leave now, so I can get this all over with," I interrupted him.

"Don't you want to say good-bye to your brother first? He should be home soon?" My mom asked.

"No, I do not want to say good-bye to my *step* brother."

"But Clint will miss you so much," My mom said trying to change my mind. I was so mad at her that I couldn't even stand the sight of her standing in front of me.

"So whether or not he says good-bye or not he will miss me and I don't care if he does," I said.

"All right, I'll tell him you said good-bye and that you will miss him."

"But I didn't say that."

"Fine, but I will miss you baby, and I love you," My mother said trying to give me a hug.

"Don't touch me!" I yelled.

"Bye Honey," My mom called out of the door as Travis was putting me in the car and Paul was putting my bags in the trunk. I just sat in the car and scowled at my mother. I hated her so much for doing this. I wanted to stay here with my friends, but I didn't mind leaving my family. They never were important in my life, so why would I miss them? "I will come and visit you soon and maybe I will bring Clint."

"Don't bother coming. I don't want you there," I said as Paul closed the car door and he drove out of my driveway.

"You don't get along with your mother too much, huh?" Travis asked stupidly.

"What do you think?" I answered.

"Why don't you?"

"I just don't. It's none of your business anyway," I told them with an attitude. I knew I was kind of being rude; they just met me and were asking reasonable questions.

"I think you'll like Long Ridge," Paul said.

"I doubt it."

"It is really nice there," Travis told me.

"Yeah it is excluded from everyone. It is in the middle of the woods, but about five miles down the road is a small town," Paul added.

"Wow, that's interesting," I said sarcastically.

"Okay," Both the guys said realizing they aren't going to get a friendly comment out of me.

"I see you are going to be a hard one to work with," Travis informed me.

"I'll try to make it hard for ya," I assured them.

"Well at least it isn't me that will be working with you," He announced.

"Who will?" I asked.

"I think Shawn and Kim. You will most likely be in their group," Paul answered.

"Group? What do you mean?"

"There are separate groups of kids. It helps keep you all in order, and it is easier for the counselors. Shawn will explain it to you. You probably will have the best leaders. Shawn is the founder of Long Ridge, and if he has to go somewhere, Kim keeps everything in order," Travis was telling me. After he stopped talking, I fell asleep instantly. I was still a high so I needed the sleep; I just had to sleep it off.

"Candace, we are here. Wake up," Paul said while he was shaking me.

"Stop shaking me, I have a killer headache and you shaking me is not helping," I said in a tired, but in loud and stern voice.

"Oh sorry, I forgot you were still high," Paul said.

"So this is it," I said as I stepped out of the car. I looked around and it was all green. Very different compared to where I came from. I inhaled and it even smelled differently, it smelled like fresh air and I didn't like it. The pine trees were blowing in the soft wind and you could hear millions of birds chirping.

"Yes, welcome to Long Ridge," A young looking dark haired man said as he was untying my hands. "Hi Candace, I am Shawn,"

"Hi," I replied miserably.

"I am Kim," This tall curly red haired lady said as she grabbed my hand to shake it.

"If you please would get your bags out of the car and come to my office I will tell you everything about Long Ridge," Shawn said.

"All right, I guess I don't really have a choice," I said.

"Here you are," Travis said as he was handing me my two bags.

"Thanks," I said in a quiet voice. I actually will admit that I liked the surroundings of this place, but I wasn't about to let all of them know that.

"Here is my office. Kim, can you leave us alone, so we can have some time to talk?" Shawn said.

"I'm sorry, but I'm not going to give any to you," I said loud enough so the people around me could hear and I noticed a few of the other students start to laugh at what I said.

"Excuse me, but I do this with all of the students; it is procedure," Shawn said walking right into my next comment.

"That is some procedure, even with the guys you do it? That's just sick."

"I didn't mean it that way. Come on in here," He ordered me grabbing my arm. The office was really dark, there was one window, but the sun wasn't shining in there. There were no lights and there were just two seats and no table and the smell was retched. It smelled as if it hadn't been occupied in years.

"This is a really crappy office," I informed him.

"I don't actually work in here, this is just where I talked to the kids if I need to."

"Oh."

"So Candace," He started.

"It is Candy. That is my nickname; that is what every one of my friends calls me, so I guess you can too."

"Well isn't that sweet of you to offer. Okay Candy, I will have to step out of the room while the doctor comes in and inspects you. We will give you some new clothes just for today, but every other day you can wear your own clothes. Also I am going to take you're bags and make sure everything in there you can have here," Shawn told me, and then the doctor came in and he left with my bags.

"Hi Candace. I am Dr. Sharon Kelly." She said to me.

"Hi," I said and I really wish I didn't have a doctor in here. Ever since I started using drugs I hated doctors. I didn't like their nosy questions. They wanted to know everything about you and they never liked the truth. Every doctor I had seen always told me to change my ways, but I figured it's my life and if I want to screw it up let me.

"I know you're going to hate this, but I have to give you a physical and inspect you, and give you new clothes for the day," She said.

"What's up with that, why can't I wear these clothes, my own?" I asked pointing at my chest.

"Because Shawn has to look at them and make sure you aren't hiding any drugs in them, besides what you are wearing now is unacceptable for this school. Also you can't have any jewelry, unless they are stud earrings," She told me while looking kind of suspicious, and I knew why she was looking at me that way. She knew I had drugs hidden with me. "Also I have to ask you a bunch of questions, but Shawn has to be around for them. Right now though you have to get changed."

"Why can't I give you the drugs I have with me and then I wouldn't have to get changed, can I do that?"

"I'm sorry, but no you can't, and remember what I said about unacceptable attire," So I had no choice, but to wear the crappy clothes that they had given me. I did not like them at all; they made me look as if I didn't have a figure. After I was getting changed, Shawn came back in.

"Okay she is all ready for our lovely questions," The doctor sarcastically said him.

"Okay, but I would like to ask her them alone. I can tell by the way that she looks that she is hiding something. She isn't going to talk about it with a doctor around, so I'll just ask the questions and then tell you if she needs any tests done. Would that be okay?" I heard Shawn whisper to her.

"Of course it is Shawn. I understand," The doctor said and then left.

"So..." Shawn said.

"So..."

"I know you're not going to enjoy these questions, but I have to ask them. It is to help you, really it is."

"Start asking, so I can get this over with."

"All right. Umm...have you been...had sexual contact anytime recently?" I could tell he was not use to asking these kinds of questions, especially to a teenage girl.

"That just had to be your first question huh? Yes I have," I said and I was kind of embarrassed for it, yet I don't know why.

"Okay how recently would that be?"

"About eight hours ago give or take a few."

"You're probably the first person that has ever admitted that."

"Well, I don't really have that much to hide. There are only a few things I don't tell people," I said and I knew he wanted me to tell him what those were, as if I would. Joel doesn't even know every thing about me.

"Okay," Shawn asked me many more questions, and he told me that all through the week I would have to have a few tests done to make sure I am healthy, like a pregnancy test and I surely wasn't too fond of that idea.

"Are we done now? I really am getting sick of talking, and I just want to relax. It is bad enough I have to be here, just let me be. You don't have to talk to me, you don't even have to help me. I don't need it, I know other people who should be here instead of me. I didn't do anything, other people did," I said as I walked out of the room.

"Candy wait. We are done with the questions, but there are other things, you won't have to talk, just listen," He assured me. Shawn actually seemed pretty easy going and nice. I never really liked teachers, I always thought they believed it was their way or no way. Shawn didn't act like that. I pictured in my head him to be the type that would sit down with you and take what you say to heart. I liked that about him.

"Fine," I said turning and walked back into the room.

"Thank you. First thing I want to tell you, is that you're not as tough as you think you are."

"Whatever," I said ignoring him.

"I need to tell you the rules. There are three main rules. The first one is, there are *no* drugs. If you get caught with them, you will be punished severely, second rule is that there is no violence. You are not to get in fights with other students here. And this rule is the one that I am really stressing for you it is that there is none, *not any sex.*"

"What?" I interrupted him.

"There is no sex allowed here, and I really don't want you to even try and break that rule. From what your mother told me, that is going to be a tough one for you to follow."

"This sucks!" I yelled, "I want to go home, where I have friends where I have a life!"

"Do you honestly think those friends are true friends? I am sorry to say this, but those two girls that you are friends with, are only friends for drugs. And that one guy Brent, why do you think he is your friend?"

"I never said Brent was a true friend of mine. I know he isn't, he only likes me for one reason and one reason only."

"Why do you do that to yourself? Did you ever think to find true friends?" Shawn asked me.

"I don't know. It is just a way of my life."

"Really?"

"Fine you got me it isn't a way of life. A while ago there was this rumor about me, it was about me having sex with every guy I see. This one guy that I was dating made that up because I broke up with him. I didn't want to have sex with him. Well he wanted to get back at me for it, cause he was never dumped, I tried telling people it was untrue, but he was the most popular guy in my school so naturally people believed him over me. It got so out of hand that I couldn't stop it, so I just made it true, and Brent was there for it," I said.

"Oh, I am sorry. What about that Joel guy?"

"No! No! No!" I yelled, "Joel is not like that to me."

"What do you mean?"

"I care about Joel, he is the only guy I actually care about. We have been friends before the rumors and drugs. Yeah, I'll admit it, he has wanted to have sex with me, but he hasn't got any, the only thing he has gotten,

21

was that we kissed, but we never went all the way. Even after I told him, I would never "do it" with him, he was still my best friend. He told me that he was glad I didn't do anything with him, he thought it would change things between us. Both of us know he was right."

"That is actually good,' Shawn told me, smiling, "Okay how Long Ridge works is, that it is a high school, we teach you as if you are in a typical school, but along with that we mainly help you get over the drug addiction. There are groups here. We have six separate groups; Oak Ridge, Maple Spring, Pine Stream, Ever Green, Birch Wood. You will meet all the counselors of these groups in time."

"That was only five groups and what group am I in?"

"You will be in the sixth group headed by Kim and me, the Spruce Falls. I will introduce you to the other students now. They should be in the front room," Shawn exclaimed.

"Okay," I said even thought I really couldn't care about meeting these people. We walked into the main room; the room was larger than any living room I have ever seen. It had a few chairs, two couches, an organ, and a few tables with lights on them, and in the front part of it there was a magnificent fireplace. Also there were stairs that went to the counselor's rooms.

"Everyone, there is a new person in our group, Candy. If you would kindly introduce yourself to her, that would be great. We can go around the room and you can say your name," Shawn told them all.

"I'm Jay," This one dark haired boy started out.

"I am AJ," This blonde girl who looked a lot like me said.

"Austin," He had blonde hair that was spiky.

"Hi I am Angela," She said her name so perky that I just wanted to hit her.

"Hey, I'm Kaitlyn."

"I'm May."

"Hello I'm Hobie," He had brown spiky hair.

"I'm Harrison," A black haired boy said.

"I am Jackson," A black guy said, he looked older than he actually was.

"And I'm Bryce," Bryce was really cute; he had kind of spiky blonde hair that was bleached. You could tell it was dyed, because you could see the dark hair at his roots, but guys look good like that; it looks like they just dyed their tips. He also had these amazing big blue eyes that almost could drill into you.

"Bryce, could you show Candy around?" Shawn asked and I was very glad when he agreed.

"Yeah sure, Shawn. Also, I want to talk to you later."

"All right buddy," Shawn answered him patting him on the back.

"Come on Candy," He said leading the way out of the building. There were a lot of other buildings that looked like cabins. It really felt like camp not a high school for screwed up kids. "So how did you end up here?"

"My mom called them and they dragged me out of my house after I got home from a party. Joel, my one friend who drove me home saw me being chased by them and he tried to stop them, but it didn't work," I explained and I was really longing to talk to Joel and tell him what happened.

"So…this Joel guy, is he your boy friend?" Bryce asked.

"No, he is my best friend though. I would say he is like a brother, but I wouldn't insult him like that."

"What do you mean?" Bryce asked looking really confused.

"Brothers suck," I told him.

"Gee thanks, I am a brother," Bryce told me and I felt really stupid with that remark.

"Oh well I'm sorry; my brother sucks. And I wouldn't want to ever think of Joel as being like him."

"Is your brother older than you?"

"Yeah, but actually he is my stepbrother, and I figured that when my mom and his dad got a divorce that I wouldn't have to see him, but every other week he comes, and I hate it."

"Most of the time older brothers pick on little sisters. I have a younger brother and before I started drugs I picked on him a lot."

"He doesn't pick on me, but I hate him."

"Oh okay," He said and then for a while we walked in silence. Nobody, not even Joel knew, but I was hiding a major secret, that I have been hiding for years. And nobody was going to find out, at least that is the way I wanted to keep it…then.

"I didn't really mean to get snobby with you and have an attitude, but I am just not really happy about being here," I apologized yet I wasn't sure why I was apologizing. I didn't do anything wrong and I didn't really sound that snobby. I think I just really wanted to hear his voice again.

"Oh it is okay, I understand," Bryce accepted it.

"Why does everyone here say they 'understand'?"

"Well Shawn always says that, because before he founded this place he was doing some heavy drugs. And I understand what it is like to be the new kid around here. Just three months ago I was the new kid. I was also dragged out of my house by Paul and Travis, so I understand what that is like," Bryce explained.

"Oh."

"Here we are, this is your room. You will be sharing it with AJ, Angel, May, and Kaitlyn."

"Joy," I said sarcastically.

"Yeah, I know it's not the greatest, but you get use to it after awhile. I share a cabin, room thing with five other guys. It isn't that bad, really it isn't."

"I have never shared a room with someone, except if I was staying at someone's house."

"The exact same thing with me. I guess we are alike in many ways," Bryce said in the hottest voice I have ever heard in my life. It just made my blood boil inside of me.

"I guess, but more so or less," I commented.

"Oh."

"How did you end up here?" I asked.

"Um...my dad got a hold of the people here, and he called them to drag me away from home. He couldn't handle me, or at least that is what he said to me."

"I'm sorry."

"It isn't that big of a deal anymore; I have been getting over it." I could tell he wasn't fully over it yet though.

"Is there only a certain time when parents can visit here?" I asked as I put my bags on my bed.

"Well, if there is an emergency at home, or there is a really good reason why they need to come then they can come whenever, but normally there is this day when all the parents come to talk to Shawn and Kim. There is usually four in one year, it's kind of like a parent teacher conference. You just missed that by three days," Bryce explained to me.

"Good."

"Why?"

"I don't really get along with my mom, especially now," I answered him.

"I get it, but I think your mom will have to come to talk to Shawn."

"That really sucks."

"In your case yep."

Bryce showed me around the whole place. It was pretty, I guess. He showed me where we eat, the boy's rooms, the rest of the girl's rooms, the woods, the river, and everything else. Then he had to take me back to where Shawn was waiting for us.

"Bryce, can you not tell Shawn anything I told you? I really don't want him knowing about me," I asked.

"Of course; it isn't even my place to tell him, it's yours," He answered as if he was a teacher.

"Thanks," I said.

"Well here you go, I will see you later I have to get back to the rest of the group," Bryce said.

"Thanks for showing her around Bryce," Shawn said as he patted Bryce on the back.

"No problem Shawn, it was my pleasure," Bryce said as he gave me one last look and went running off. I really liked Bryce, but not how I liked the other guys I have known. I liked him, I really liked him.

"I think he has a crush on you," Shawn said smiling.

"How do you figure?" I said in my mad voice. I didn't have the same voice as I did with Bryce, but only because I didn't want Shawn to think I was happy about being here.

"I think that, because he has never enjoyed me asking him to show someone around, and he didn't seem to mind it this time."

"Oh," I said and I have to admit I was happy about hearing that. I was trying to hold back a smile and it wasn't working too well.

"Did Bryce show you everywhere?"

"Yeah he did."

"Okay good," Shawn said looking around. "Well, it is dinnertime, so I'll take you to the cafeteria and we can get something to eat."

"Okay, but I really am not that hungry," I said. I really don't eat that much, when I did eat a lot I felt really fat.

"Are you anorexic?" Shawn asked concerned.

29

"No, I am not. I just don't eat every meal. I do eat though," I answered mad that he would even ask that.

"What about bulimic?"

"No. I just don't eat all of the time, but I don't starve myself, or throw-up my food. That is just gross. I don't have a big appetite...that's all."

"Okay I was just checking. But you do have to eat everything we give you."

"Why?" I asked thinking this sucks.

"Because we do have people who are anorexic and bulimic."

"So that isn't my problem," I said to him.

"You're right, it isn't you're problem, but if they see you not eating a lot they will think that is unfair that you don't have to eat everything."

"That's stupid, just because you don't want me doing drugs doesn't mean that I'd expect everyone else to be banned from them."

"Nice try, but next time you try and get your way don't go using a scenario that involves something no one is allowed to do." Right then I knew I was never going to get my way in this school.

"Fine, but what if I don't like what you give me?"

"Pretend you do."

"This sucks."

"I know I hear that all the time from you kids, but you have to," Shawn took me into the cafeteria. "Here is the one table for your group. But if you don't want to sit with anyone today you can sit over there," He pointed to a table by one of the windows. "Or for you're first day you can sit with anyone you want."

"I'll sit there," I said pointing to the seat that was excluded from everyone else.

"Okay, you want me to sit with you."

"No," I said thinking, why would I want a teacher to sit with me?

"Okay, just was asking. Let's get dinner."

"All right," I said having Shawn lead me to the counter with all this food on it. I took a piece of chicken, some carrots, a salad (which looked horrible) and a glass of water. "Don't you have any pop?" I asked.

"No."

"Okay fine," I said walking over to the table that Shawn said I could sit at.

Chapter 2

I was sitting there for awhile daydreaming and moving the food around on my plate when I heard a familiar voice behind me say, "Hey can I sit here?" I turned around and say Bryce.

"Oh hi Bryce. Did Shawn tell you to come over here to make sure I eat everything?" I asked.

"No."

"Okay you can sit here then."

"You don't eat?" He asked.

"Yeah I do, I just don't have a very big appetite."

"Oh okay. You should eat at least a little."

"I know I should, but I am not hungry at all. I am too depressed to eat."

"Okay, well then get happy!" He said smiling and I couldn't help from smiling.

"Is there a phone I can use?" I asked.

"You actually have to ask Shawn if you can use the phone."

"Okay, I will then," I got up and walked over to Shawn and tapped him on the shoulder.

"Yes Candy?" He asked.

"Can I use the phone? I need to call a friend of mine that was there when Travis and Paul took me away. And he is probably wondering what happened."

"Sure have Bryce show you where the phone is," I walked back over to Bryce.

"What he won't let you?" Bryce asked.

"No, he said I could, but can you please show me where it is?"

"Yeah sure," He said as he got up and led the way. "So who do you need to call?" He asked.

"Joel. I need to tell him that I am okay, he's probably worried sick about me." We walked outside and went into the main lodge.

"Here it is," He said pointing to a tiny table that was hidden in the corner. "I will just wait over here so you can have at least a little privacy."

"Thanks," I said in the sweetest voice. I dialed Joel's number and his mom answered. His mom doesn't like me so I have to disguise my voice. "Hi, may I please speak to Joel?"

"Yeah hold on," Joel's mom said in a tired voice, but I figured she was probably drunk.

"Hello," Joel said.

"Hi Joel it's…"

"Candy!" He interrupted.

"Yeah hey."

"Where are you?" Joel asked yelling.

"Did you ever hear of the school Long Ridge?"

"Yeah isn't that where druggies go if they get caught?"

"Yeah, or if their mother calls them to take you there."

"Your mom did that to you?" He screamed as if I couldn't hear him.

"Joel you don't have to scream in my ear."

"Oh sorry, it is just my mom is yelling in the back round."

"Oh I figured that is who it was."

"Yeah. Brent came over just a little bit ago, asking where you were."

"Oh. Is he okay?" I asked wondering why he would go all the way to Joel's house just to get a hold of me.

"Yeah, like I said he was looking for you, so you can figure out what he wanted."

"Oh surprise, surprise. That is the only reason he likes me."

"I thought you always knew that?"

"I did, I just didn't want it to be true."

"Is your mom going to be coming to see you soon?"

"I don't know, why?"

"Because I want to see you."

"Well, go and see her later, and ask her to come. Tell her I said the only way she can come is if she brings you?"

"Okay do you want Brent to come?"

"Sure tell her to bring Brent too. I got to go. I don't know how long I am allowed to be on the phone for," I told Joel and looked back at Bryce who was leaning up against the wall looking down at the floor.

"Okay well I'll tell your mom to bring us tomorrow," Joel said.

"All right I'll see you tomorrow."

"Love ya, Candy girl."

"Love you too Joel," I said and hung up the phone. "Okay I am done," I said to Bryce.

"Okay, I may be a bit nosy, but who is Brent and why does he only like you for one reason?" I just started laughing.

"Brent is this guy I know, and he wants *some*," I said hoping he would get it.

"Huh?"

"Okay I don't want to come right out and say it so I'll explain it. A guy I know, not a friend or lover, but a guy I know and hang out with, wanted some from a girl, like me," I said.

"Oh he want *some*."

"Yeah."

"You do that?"

"I did, but from what I found out it is a rule that I can't do that."

"Oh yeah, since Shawn caught two kids doing that he has really knuckled down on that rule. Also, he really stresses that rule to certain people."

"I see I am one of those people."

"I guess so," He said, "Did you say to Joel c-ya tomorrow?"

"Yeah he is going to make my mom bring him and Brent."

"Oh, you and Brent aren't going to…"

"I doubt it, I can guarantee he will try though."

"That isn't good is it?"

"Not really. That is why I need your help."

"Huh?"

"Can you like please hang out with me all of tomorrow, so Brent doesn't get any ideas?"

"Sure, I also want to meet this Joel guy."

"Okay, Joel is really cool. You should get along with him. He usually gets along with anyone."

"I'm sure I will."

"Shawn told me something and I was wondering if it was true."

"What?"

"Umm…he said…was saying that he thought…he said that you must have a crush on me."

"Where did he get that idea?"

"He said you usually don't like showing people around, but this time you didn't seem to mind, was it true?" When it comes to truth I am the person who will say it. If I am wondering something I'll just come right out and say it.

"Well I don't know, I just met you."

"Okay I was just wondering that's all."

"Oh wow it is already 10:30; we are late."

"For what?"

"We are supposed to be in our rooms at 10 except on weekends."

"We have a curfew?"

"Yep. I'll walk you to your room."

"Okay," We walked to my cabin/room type of thing.

"Well here you are.   I will see you tomorrow at 7:30."

"AM? Jeez, well thanks, thanks a lot."

"For what?"

"For everything, showing me around and for what you are doing for me tomorrow."

"You're welcome for everything."

"Well I'll see you tomorrow at 7:30 in the early, early morning. I can't believe that."

"Night," Bryce said, smiled that great smile of his, and then walked away. I had to admit I really, really like being here, but only because my mom, and brother weren't here and Bryce was here.

"So do you have a good first day here?" One of the girls asked, but I couldn't remember who it was. I only could remember May; she was the black girl you looked a lot older than we were.

"It could have been better. I could have been with friends."

"Yeah I know what you mean, ever since I got here I have wanted to leave," May said.

"I wish you were at home and never came here," One of the girls said to me. She was the one who looked a lot like me.

"Why?" I asked.

"Because you are stealing my man."

"Who?"

"Bryce, hello who else?"

"He didn't mention anything about you, so you must not be that important to him," I said in a snotty voice and laid down on my bed. "He especially didn't mention you while we were doing it. All I heard was him yelling my name," I joked and had the biggest grin on my face. I have become the type of person whom if you bother me or say something to me that I don't like I'll say something right back. Sometimes that does get me in trouble, because I can only fight with my words I was not at all strong.

"I am more important to him than he thinks."

"Oh so you mean you just want him to be your guy, but you aren't a couple."

"You and him seriously did it?" The girl that didn't like me asked.

"No, I don't work that fast, but I do like him," I said.

"Stay away from him," She ordered me; I just made this face as if I was scared, but she could tell I was being sarcastic.

39

"Bryce doesn't even like her," Another one of the girls commented.

"Shut up Angela!"

"I don't like being called Angela. You know that AJ."

"Okay fine, Angel."

"Thanks Angel for saying your name and AJ's name. I had no idea who all of you were," I said.

Angel had short dirty blonde hair, green eyes, and she was medium height.

"Oh you're welcome. We introduced ourselves before."

"I wasn't really paying much attention to you all."

"Okay, I don't blame you," The one girl said.

"So why are you in here anyway?" AJ asked. AJ had medium length bleach blonde hair (like me) blue eyes, and she was just a bit taller than I was.

"I killed three people," I said sarcastically. "I want you all to know this, I don't want to be here, I don't make friends with girls, unless they are friends for drugs, as far as I know I don't like any of you. I don't plan on telling any of you my problems, how I got here, or anything having to do with my life. I also don't plan on any of you telling me anything about you, cause I don't care. And AJ you snap at me again about Bryce or anything I swear I won't even think twice about beating the living crap out of you," I said which was a bluff.

"I already like you. I think we will be getting along great," The other girl that I believe was Kaitlyn.

"Kaitlyn right?"

"Yeah but everyone calls me Kaye, we will get along great we both hate people," She said. Kaye had black hair, brown eyes and pale skin, but not really pale.

"Okay, but I don't hate people. I just hate everyone here," I said.

"Yeah except Bryce I see," She said and smiled toward AJ. "AJ, I see you have some competition."

"Oh shut up!" AJ yelled.

"Yeah, I think we will be getting along," I said. I had to say that Kaye was cool.

"Come on guys we need to get to bed now, Kim will be around checking up on us to make sure we are sleeping," May said as she turned out the lights.

Chapter 3

I woke up the next morning to Angel yelling at us to get up. I had a horrible stiff neck and hurt back from the mattress and pillows.

"Ouch," I said to myself rubbing the back of my neck.

"I know it hurts, but you'll get used to it," Angel said perky.

"Hopefully."

"Candace, a few people are here to see you they're in Shawn's office," Kim said. I jumped out of bed got changed, fixed my hair, put make-up on, and ran out the door to Shawn's office in record time.

"Oh and Kim my name is Candy," I yelled to her as I was running out the door.

"Candy wait up," I heard someone yell.

"Oh hey Bryce," I said slowing down.

"Where you going so fast?"

"Joel is here," I answered starting to run again with him behind me.

"Oh is he that good of a friend?"

"The best," I answered him.

"Candy girl!" Joel yelled running to me. He gave me a huge hug lifting me up in the air.

"Hey Joel."

"Hi Candy."

"Brent hey, I didn't think you would actually come," I said giving him a hug.

"Why would I turn down a chance to see you?"

"I didn't think you would have the time to come."

"I'd make the time for you," He said making me smiling. Even though he only liked me for one reason I had to admit he was charming.

"Yeah real big time about a half-hour," Joel joked.

"Don't say that around here, I already got ragged on about that."

"From who?" Brent asked.

"See that guy over there?" I said pointing to Shawn.

"Yeah," They both answered.

"Him," I said.

"Do you have a hug for me?" A voice said that made me shiver. It was Clint my stepbrother.

"Hi Clint," I said as he reached out his arms for me to give him a hug, and just to be polite I did hug him. It made me feel weird though.

"Mom said I can come here once a week to see you," Clint said.

"You can't," I answered hoping that he would believe me.

"Why not?" He asked.

"People are only allowed to visit at certain times," I told him. Joel looked really mad. He knew that I hated Clint being around me, Joel didn't trust him, either did I.

"Oh that is too bad. I hate the idea of not being able to see you all the time," All I could think was I'm not. But I just nodded. "Do you feel the same?" He asked.

"Yeah," I lied. Clint thought I liked him as much as he liked me, which I didn't. And I wasn't in the mood to fight about it with him. Clint and I have never fought, but I have fought with him in my head, so many times I have wanted to start yelling at him.

"So who is this?" Brent asked pointing at Bryce. I could tell that Brent was jealous.

"This is Bryce. He has been nice enough to show me around and make me fit in. Bryce this is Joel and Brent," I pointed to each of them.

"And I am Clint, Candace's brother. And if you lay a finger on this girl I swear I will rip you to pieces, she is mine," Clint said shaking Bryce's hand and pulling him close to whisper that to him, but I could hear. Bryce had a nervous look on his face. It was probably because Clint was a strong looking guy.

"Leave him alone Clint, and I hate it when you say I am yours," I said in a different tone of voice that I have never had with Clint.

"You talking back to me?" Clint asked.

"Yeah," I said.

"Come with me. I need to talk to you alone," Clint said grabbing my arm tightly, but the others couldn't tell that he was hurting me.

"I will be right back guys," I said to them with Clint almost dragging me away.

"What was that about, you never talk back to me?" Clint asked.

"I just didn't like you talking to Bryce that way," I answered feeling nervous.

"You know I love you, and I just want to look out for you," Clint said trying to kiss me. And not kiss me like on the cheek, kiss me like how Brent has kissed me.

"No," I said turning my head away, so he couldn't kiss me.

"Don't you ever say no to me!" Clint yelled and the grabbed my shoulder and made me kiss him. That was my secret, Clint. He was not a nice brother; he was a controlling, demanding, asshole.

"Stop I will scream, so people will hear me," I said struggling to get away from him.

"You wouldn't do that," Clint said.

"You want to bet," I said and tried to yell, but Clint put his hand over my mouth and shoved me to the ground.

"Come on we have to get back to everyone," He said pulling me up from the ground, "And if you tell anyone about this, they will be so disappointed in you for doing this," I made the mistake of believing him for years, and I still did. We walked back to the guys and I saw that AJ was hitting on Joel. For some reason seeing her with him bothered me, but then I noticed he wasn't paying any attention to her.

"Okay we're back," I said as if nothing happened.

"When are you going to be coming back home?" Joel asked with Brent nodding.

"Actually Shawn never told me that. Do you know Bryce?" I asked.

"Usually it is about four years, unless he doesn't believe you are ready to go back out into 'The Real World' as he calls it," Bryce exclaimed.

"Four years?" Brent questioned.

"Yep," Bryce answered.

"What am I supposed to do till then?" Brent really was selfish, he didn't care about me having to be in here for four years, he just cared that he wasn't going to be able to do it with me till then.

"Get another girl Brent," I said kind of mad at him for thinking that way and he could tell that I was very mad at him.

"You're mad at me?" He said as a question.

"Yeah I am, you don't care that I am going to be suffering in here for four years. All you care about is how you won't be able to "do it" with me."

"I'm sorry. I will miss you and I care about you."

"No you don't Brent. I could tell you that I would never have sex with you again and you wouldn't talk to me ever again. Caring is like how Joel is, Joel will miss me and he cares about me. He knows that I won't "do it" with him and yet he still hangs around with me. So Brent don't say you care about me, you only care about what I will do for you and with you, that is all," I said.

"Good-job," Shawn said behind me.

"Oh Shawn I didn't realize you were behind me."

"You have just past the first test."

"What was it?" I asked.

"It was what you just said to Brent. There isn't a certain test you past. There is a different one for each person," Shawn explained.

"Whoa, I actually passed a test," I said smiling. I have never passed a test in my life. Well, at least not tests like that.

"It feels good to do something right, doesn't it?" Shawn asked.

"It isn't something to celebrate about, but it was okay," I said, but in my mind I knew I was lying to him. I did feel really good about it.

"Candy can I please talk to you alone?" Joel asked.

"Sure Joel," I answered. "Shawn can I take him to my room, we won't do anything...I promise."

"I don't think…"

"Come on Shawn she promised, you will have to trust her sometime," Kim said walking towards us.

"Oh alright, thanks to Kim you can," He gave in.

"Thanks Shawn," I wasn't about to say thank you to Kim, I didn't like her. She was trying to be nice and get on my good side, but it was just an act. I knew she didn't like me being here very much, or at least that is what I thought. I took Joel to my room with Bryce following me. When we got to my room Bryce waited outside. AJ and Kaye were in there. "Can you two please leave?" I asked.

"We could, but we're not," AJ said as Kaye was getting up to leave.

"Please?" I asked.

"Not a chance," She answered.

"Bryce is outside of here," I said trying to persuade her.

"It's not going to work."

"Bryce!" I called.

"Yeah?" He came in.

"Do you know any other rooms or places we can talk?" I asked.

"Sure you can use my room," He answered.

49

"Thanks Bryce." I winked at him and then added, "Maybe we'll talk in *your* room later." Bryce knew I was kidding and that nothing would happen. While we were walking out of the room AJ gave me the meanest look while Kaye was laughing hysterically.

"AJ is a…" He stopped, so Joel finished it for him.

"A bitch."

"Right," He joked, but I think he agreed. "Here you are," When we walked in Austin, Jackson and Harrison were there.

"You want us to leave huh?" Jackson said.

"Please if you could, I need to talk to my friend and AJ wouldn't leave my room," I said.

"Sure it is okay," Austin said, as Jackson was about to say no.

"Thanks guys," I said.

"Anything for a beautiful damsel in distress," Austin said. So the three guys, plus Bryce left leaving us alone. We sat down on someone's bed.

"So what's up? Why did you need to talk to me alone?" I asked.

"Well, one I know you are not allowed to have drugs, but I figured you would need a

50

smoke sometime, so here are some cigarettes," He said handing me a pack of them.

"Thanks Joel that is about the best gift someone could give me while I am here."

"Also I wanted you to know that I know what Clint has been doing to you," He said and I was in shock.

"What do you mean, doing to me?" I asked softly with my voice cracking.

"Him being aggressive to you, like today him pushing you. I followed you and saw him push you to the ground," He said and all I was hoping was that he didn't know that Clint kissed me.

"That is all you saw right?" I asked.

"Yeah, wait, did he do something else?" Joel asked furious.

"Oh yeah, that's it. I meant to say were you the only one who saw, right? It just didn't come out of my mouth like that."

"Well I know you are lying to me, but I can't force you to tell me anything," Joel said. He was very good with telling when I am lying.

"You're not going to tell anyone are you? Nobody will believe us and plus they will keep me here longer than four years then," I asked almost praying out loud that he wouldn't go blabbing to people.

"As much as I want to tell people I won't. I'll let you do that when you are ready," He answered.

"Thanks Joel," I said and gave him a hug.

"Come on, that Shawn guy will start getting ideas," He said and grabbed my hand. We walked outside and Bryce was still waiting there for us.

"You two ready?" He asked.

"Yep," I answered.

"Wait Bryce; I want you to do me a favor," Joel said.

"Yeah sure, what?"

"Keep an eye on my Candy girl here," He said as he put his arm around me. "She is a good kid and I want you to watch out for her, please do that for me. I want to make sure she is in good hands."

"Sure, I will" Bryce said.

"You are a lucky guy, you get to hang out with her for four years. Trust me it will be fun," Joel said shaking Bryce's hand. It was as if they were making a deal. We walked back where Shawn and Kim were. Brent must have gone back to the car, and my mom and Clint were standing there talking to Shawn.

"Oh hi Hun, how are you hanging in there?" My mom asked. I didn't answer her; I didn't want to have big fight in front of all these people, so I figured I wouldn't talk to her at all. "Do you like it here Candace?" And when I didn't answer again she started yelling at me. "Candace you never ignore me, when I ask you something you answer. Now how do you like it here?"

"Oh I love it mom," I said sarcastically, "You wanna know the best part? I am away from you and your stupid questions! What do you think I'm going to fall in love with this place when I am away from my friends and I have no life anymore!" I screamed.

"You shouldn't talk to Mom that way," Clint said sternly.

"Oh stay out of it, Clint. She wanted me to answer, so I did," I yelled at him.

"You should never speak that disrespectful to your mother," Clint said.

"One Clint, you can't tell me what to do. I think you belong here more than I do. And two, if you don't want me talking that way to Mom, I'll start talking like that to you. Okay you prick?" Clint didn't say anything, either did anyone else. Everyone was in shock, especially my mom she has never seen me even raise my voice to Clint.

"Okay on that happy note, I have to get home, so Mrs. Walkinson are we going to be leaving soon?" Joel asked. I knew he was saying that get my so-called-family out of there and to leave me alone.

"Oh yes Joel, you can go wait with Brent in the car," My mom said.

"Bye my Candy girl, and hey Bryce you're a cool guy," Joel said to Bryce and gave me a hug. "Kid behave so you can get out soon," He told me and then walked away to the car.

"I am so sorry to have to bring Candace here. This is probably hard for you, she just doesn't behave or do anything good. I just had to get her away. I also am sorry for that scene my daughter just made," My mom said and I couldn't believe it. I never do anything good, well then what does that say about her; she raised me.

"Don't call me your daughter, not after what you just said to him. I don't want to even be considered a family member to you. Don't come back here, I never want to see you again,

Mrs. Walkinson," I said to my mom and walked away. I walked back to my room. It wasn't just AJ and Kaye, there was Angel and one of the guys, Jay.

"What was all the noise out there?" Kaye asked.

"It was my mom, my stepbrother, and me fighting," I told her.

"Oh was your stepbrother that really hot guy you brought in here?" AJ asked.

"No that was my best friend Joel, Clint was the guy I was walking back with while you were *trying* to hit on Joel," I answered.

"Trying you mean succeeding on hitting on him."

"If you call that succeeding I'd hate to think what failing would be, because you suck at it," I said calmly as if I wasn't even fighting with her.

"What do you mean? He likes me."

"HA! Joel like you, yeah right. He called you a bitch when you wouldn't let us use the room."

"Well it didn't seem as if he hated me when we were talking."

"Don't you mean you talking and him not saying anything," Kaye said making me laugh.

55

"He was talking and looking me over."

"No he wasn't talking and he wasn't staring at you, he was looking beyond you where Candy went. And then to make it even more funny, he walked away when you were talking to him," Kaye said.

"Yeah, let me tell you AJ he must really like you," I said sarcastically.

"Whatever, I know when a guy is flirting with me," AJ said as if she had the knowledge of everything.

"You may know that, but I have known Joel my whole life and I know how he flirts. One he pays attention to every word someone says. Two he touches the girl, like he holds her hand or puts his arms around the girl's waist. And three, he has never walked away from anyone while they were talking to him, unless the person is boring him to death or he really hates the person. Yep that puts you at the top of his list on girls he wants to date," I said laughing and making everyone else in the room laugh too.

"Shut up, just shut up! My life was perfect till you came."

"Perfect? If you're life was so perfect than you wouldn't be here," I remarked.

"Why don't you just go back to that dump you came from?" She screamed at me.

"Gladly, just get me ride and fine I'll leave, but even with me gone you're not going to get Bryce, get over him. It probably isn't even your fault he doesn't like you, it may be his fault on not liking your type of girls," I said and just realized that was kind of a nice comment. "Oh my God, I was just nice, I have been here too long, get me out of here I don't like being nice."

"Wow you actually were nicer to me," AJ said surprised as I was.

"Don't get used to it," I announced. "I have a question, when will each of you be leaving here?"

"Well, all of us Spruce Falls girls will be graduating when you do, except for May. Most of the guys will be leaving, Austin, Hobie, and Bryce will be graduating with you and the rest of us. The rest will be leaving this year in about two months," Kaye told me.

"Yeah we will be having a really big party/dance thing for them a day before they leave," Angel told me, "And our parents are allowed to come a week before that."

"Joyous day there," I said sarcastically.

"I don't like it when our parents come either," Angel said.

"What is wrong with your parents?" I asked.

"Well I used to be anorexic, and it was because of my mother. She wanted me to be as thin as I could be. But whenever she comes she seems disappointed in my weight. She always asks if I have been eating a lot, which in her mind means 'you look fat, stop eating'," She explained.

"Oh sorry," I said.

"It's okay."

"Why would you care? She is just a stupid spoiled brat," AJ commented.

"Oh like you are."

"Shut up," AJ yelled.

"What has she done to you, to make you hate her?" I asked.

"Nothing, I just don't like how she acts like she is perfect."

"Since she hasn't done anything to you, I don't think you should say anything to her. It isn't her fault her mother acts like that. And even if she was spoiled, that also isn't her fault. It is just people like her and give her a lot of things. Something you'll never have. So till she does something to you, don't talk about her or I'll make it so you won't ever talk again," I said and AJ went walking out slamming the door behind her.

"Thanks Candy, no one has ever stood up for me before," Angel said.

"I would have done that no matter what. I hate that girl so much," I said as Kim walked in.

"Candy, I need to have a few words with you about AJ," Kim said looking very mad.

"What about her?" I asked.

"She told me you threatened her, is that true?" Kim asked.

"In the matter of speaking I did, but I wouldn't be able to do anything to her. She could beat me up before I even hit her once."

"Even so there is no threatening here, you will have to be punished and talk to Shawn about it," She told me.

"Oh fun fun, second day I am here I get in trouble. Nothing new," I said.

"Wait Kim!" Angel called while Kim was leading me out the door. "Candy was sticking up for me. AJ was calling me names and being mean to me again so Candy just yelled back at her for it," Angel explained.

"Still it was uncalled for her to threaten AJ," Kim said leading me out the door and across the school grounds to Shawn's office, but not the one that I was in before. It was the office that he actually works in.

"What's up Candy?" He asked me as I walked into his office and then he noticed Kim was behind me and I could tell he knew I did something wrong.

"She told me to come here to get my punishment," I told him pointing to Kim.

"What did she do?" He asked Kim.

"She threatened AJ," She answered.

"Okay Kim, you can just leave her here," He said and then Kim left. "Sit down Candy," He told me pointing to a chair in front of his desk and as I sat down there was a knock at the door. "Come in," Bryce walked in with Kim.

"Another troublemaker we have here," Kim said.

"What happened with him?" Shawn asked.

"He was yelling and swearing at AJ."

"Two in one day," Shawn answered. "Okay maybe you should go talk to AJ, and ask what is up with her, Kim."

"Alright," She said and left again.

"I think you should realize it isn't us. AJ is the one with the problem," I said. Bryce was looking at me confused.

"Shawn, there is a phone call for you," The secretary told Shawn.

"I'll be right back you two," He said.

"Why are you in here?" Bryce asked.

"About the same reason you are here," Bryce just looked at me confused. "AJ and I got in a fight and I threatened her."

"You wouldn't be able to do anything to her. She could probably even hurt me. I think she would be able to kill you."

"Exactly, I told Kim that I wouldn't be able to hurt her, but still that stupid lady brought me here for punishment," I told him.

"She really isn't that bad. I actually used to have a crush on her when I first came here, but that was only because I really couldn't stand any of the girls here. Then, I went out or rather became Angel's boyfriend, till I broke up with her, for no reason at all. But then, hey, I only went out with her because I missed making out with girls and she seemed like the only one I could take advantage of," Bryce said and he went on and on about them being a couple. I

61

wasn't really listening to the rest of what he said.

"Do you still miss making out with girls?" I just had to ask him that.

"Ha, Ha, um…well at times yes, but not so bad that I would get a girlfriend just to make out with her. Why do you ask?" He said looking at me suspicious.

"Well, I can't lie to you, I miss it. But also I am used to getting so much attention in my life by guys that it just seems as if no one even realizes I am here, or even sees me here," I said.

"I see you and I sure do realize you are here, but then so does AJ, so that may not be a great complement," He said laughing.

"From you I'll take it as a complement," I said giving him the smile that makes every guy I liked, like me back. I think it was working on him too.

"Sorry for the interruption," Shawn said walking back in. He looked a little stressed or worried, Bryce noticed it too.

"You all right Shawn?" He asked.

"Yeah I'm fine, but let us get back to your encounters with AJ. So we'll start with Candy, what happened?" He asked.

"Well what happened with her was that I came here. Since the minute she saw me she hated me, and she has been giving me attitude and being a bitch."

"There is no swearing Candy."

"Whatever sorry, but she started yelling at Angel and calling her names, so I didn't want her taking the madness of me and her out on Angel. So then I yelled back at her," I said.

"And you also..."

"Yes Shawn the answer to all your questions, I did threaten her, but both her and I know that I wouldn't be able to do anything to her. She just went running out of the room to get me in trouble. I can tell you Shawn I will be in here a lot more because she won't stop getting me in trouble till she gets me kicked out of here."

"One Candy, I will never kick you out, and two why did she start getting mad at you?"

"Because of him," I said pointing at Bryce.

"Me? Why? What did I do?" Bryce asked surprised.

"Because, she always thought you were going to be her boyfriend. Then when I came here you were spending so much time with me;

63

she felt like you rejected her," I said staring into his bright blue eyes.

"That is so stupid," Bryce said shaking his head.

"Why is it so stupid, Bryce?" Shawn asked.

"Well, because I never hang out with her or even given her ideas that I like her. But the biggest reason is that I told her flat out before, that I never liked her, because of the way she acted to people and that I would never go out with her in my life," Bryce explained.

"Okay Bryce, now that I have heard Candy's story I want to her what happened to you," Shawn said.

"Well, I was just walking around talking to Hobie when AJ came up and started yelling at me. She was saying 'why aren't you with your beloved Candy, since you like her so much,' and also she was yelling at me even more about stupid stuff. I just wasn't going to stand there and let her yell at me for no apparent reason so I yelled back and told her to keep her big, fucking mouth closed, then maybe she wouldn't be such a bitch. Excuse my language Shawn, and then Kim came over and brought me here," Bryce said, "Shawn, if you punish us for something she did to us then I have lost all respect for you."

"Well, seeing as it wasn't technically your fault I won't give you a punishment. But don't be too happy, I want you guys to do me a favor."

"What?" Bryce and I asked at the same time.

"Well, just don't be seen with each other for a few days."

"Wait, no you can't do that. I thought we weren't getting punished. That is so stupid," I said and Bryce jumped out of his seat to yell at Shawn, but I opened my mouth first.

"It is to get you and AJ to get along," He told me.

"In other words, she wins. Shawn, no matter what you do I don't like her and I never will like her. She is a bitch and all she wants is to get me away from Bryce. Which means she has just won. I will not let that happen. I don't take losing well, and that is because I haven't ever lost. So don't think this will make everything better, you can not do this," I ordered.

"Let's put it this way, if you two don't stay away from each other for, how about 5 days, then you will be punished," Shawn said, "I really want you to get along with AJ."

"Fine I will do it, but only because I don't want Bryce to get in trouble with you over something between me and AJ. I swear though, if AJ starts bragging about how she got Bryce away from me I will hit her. Even though I have never hurt a person; but I heard there is a first time for everything," I said and just as Shawn was going to yell at me for that I walked out of his office over to the main lodge, where Kaye and Angel were.

"What happened?" Angel asked.

"I seriously *hate* AJ!" I yelled as I plopped myself down on the couch next to Kaye.

"Well we knew that, but what did Shawn say?" Kaye asked.

"He told me I wasn't allowed to go near Bryce for 5 days," I said, "He is as bad as Kim is. Do you realize that AJ started yelling at Bryce, so Bryce yelled back and Kim brought him in there for punishment?"

"Really? I always thought Kim was the easy going one," Angel commented.

"No, Shawn was, till he said that if I was seen near Bryce we would be punished."

"You will be punished if you see him?"

"Yeah, I will. I hate this place more and more."

"That is absurd," Austin said from behind me.

"What is? That I hate this place?" I asked.

"No that you will be punished," He said.

"It isn't even like you were caught making out or something. Does Bryce even like you like that?" Angel added.

"I'm not sure," I answered.

"He does. All he could talk about was you. He kept all of the guys, including me, up last night till about 1 AM talking about you," Austin said.

"Really?" I said with a smile.

"Yeah, really."

"My God, you haven't even been here a week and you got a guy. You are good and you got to teach me how you do it," Angel said.

"Thank you except I don't know how I did it," I said amazed.

"Okay, but you got to know how you can get guys so easily," Angel said.

"Well, at home it is different, but not with him. He isn't like those other guys," I said recalling the guys I have slept with at home.

They were drunks and drug dealers or just guys who slept with anyone around. They were basically me.

"Oh okay I know what you mean, on how he is different," Angel said and Kaye nodded in agreement.

"He isn't like most of the guys around," Kaye added.

"I am going back to our room," I said remembering I still had the smokes from Joel that I had to hide somewhere.

"We'll join you," Kaye said.

"Why?" I asked.

"Well, I don't want you to get in trouble again, so just in case AJ comes into the room, we'll hold you back," Angel explained.

"The reason I'm coming with you is because I want to be there when you go all out on AJ," Kaye added.

"Okay," I said. We walked back to our room. When we walked in I flopped down on my bed pulling the cigarettes out of my pocket.

"Where did you get those?" Kaye asked.

"Joel brought them for me. Does Kim or Shawn look under the mattresses here?" I asked hoping I could hide them under there.

"Umm...not unless they have a suspicion that you have drugs, then they tear up the whole room looking for them," Kaye answered.

"Okay, well then I won't give them the suspicion," I answered and placed the cigarettes under my mattress. I started to unpack my bags my mom packed for me. I saw that she packed me clothes, pictures of her, Joel, Brent, and Clint. "Well, I'll just have to burn this picture," I said to no one in general.

"What is it?" Angel asked.

"It is a picture of Clint" I answered.

"Oh," My mom also packed me my diary, which was good; at least I could write my feelings down.

"Is that your diary?" Angel asked.

"Yeah, please tell me that Kim and Shawn don't read them," I said.

"No they try to respect our privacy, but don't let AJ see it, she'll take it," Kaye warned and just then AJ walked in.

"Good point, thanks," I answered and as I was flipping through the pages I noticed that my pen was on the page of my last entry. I took the pen out and turned the page and started writing-

Dear Diary,

I can't believe this diary; my mother has sent me to this stupid school

'Long Ridge' she wants me to get help here. Like to learn how to stop using drugs, and having sex with every guy I come across. I know someone who belongs here more than I do, and you know who I am talking about, S/B. There are two good things about being here.

One reason is, I can get away from my past. From my past I only miss Joel, and drugs. Joel is so so great; he brought me some cigarettes. Thank the Lord he did. I have to admit that I am glad to get rid of Brent, and my family the most.

The other reason I like it here is, that there is this really cute guy, Bryce. He has dark hair that is bleached, puppy dog blue eyes, and his smile is the greatest thing I have ever laid my eyes on. His smile just makes me melt. I didn't think a guy could look as good as he does. He is also so nice; he doesn't like me for what I can give him, like Brent does. He is so sweet too. I think I may really like him and it's not for the reasons I liked Brent; I didn't even really like Brent at all. I never met a guy like Bryce before, he makes me feel special inside, I really do think I am in love with him.

Even though there are good things here, there is one really bad thing that makes me want to go home. It is this girl named AJ. She is such a bitch; because of her I am not allowed to see Bryce for a week. She got Bryce and me in trouble with Shawn (the head guy of this place) and he told us that if he caught Bryce and me together, he would punish us. Even though, I think that is punishment enough. But I didn't want to get Bryce in trouble, so I agreed not to see him. Shawn thinks that him splitting Bryce and me up is going to make me get along with AJ, well it is making me hate her even more. Speak of the bitch, AJ just walked out of the bathroom and sat down on her bed next to me. I hate this place, even though I like Bryce. I even love his name. Well I am going to go, and probably fight with AJ again, but I swear if she says anything about her getting Bryce and me apart, I am going to slap her. Well, if I survive tomorrow I will write to you then or sometime soon. BUH~BYES.

Luv ya,
Candy

I went back to my unpacking, and when AJ
went back into the bathroom I put my diary
under my mattress with the cigarettes. The last
thing I pulled out of my bag was a letter from
my mother. I didn't feel like reading it now, so
I placed in on the table next to my bed. AJ
then walked in from the bathroom again with a
smile on her face.

"What are you so happy about?" Kaye
asked and AJ didn't answer.

"Hello she asked you a question," Angel
called to her.

"Well I don't think I should brag about it,"
AJ said and right then I knew she was smiling
about me not being able to be near Bryce.

"Don't even," I said shaking my head.

"Well, in that case; HA, HA, HA! It
worked, I knew Shawn wouldn't let you be
near Bryce after that. I won, you lost and
Bryce is mine, and he will always be mine. He
was only being nice to you, did you honestly
think he liked you. Since the day we met, we

had something between us, and he wants to extend it," AJ bragged.

"From the way he acts I bet he agrees that there should be something between you two," I said and when AJ nodded I had to add something in, "Like a continent."

"You bitch!" AJ yelled and jumped at me, knocking me into the table and she just started hitting me. "You are the worst thing that ever walked on this planet!" She screamed as I was trying to get away from her, but I couldn't move my arm. I saw that Angel went running out of the room and about a minute later Shawn, Kim, and Bryce came running back in there with her.

"AJ!" Kim yelled.

"Candy!" Bryce yelled running over to me, pulling AJ off of me and almost throwing her into the wall. "Oh my God are you alright?" He asked looking so worried.

"No, I can't move my arm and it hurts so bad. Also my head hurts real bad," I said as Shawn came over.

"Bryce, can you walk her to my office and put her on the couch, while I take care of some business here? Also don't let her fall asleep she may have a concussion," Shawn ordered

Bryce. Bryce helped me stand up, but as soon as he let go I almost fell, but he caught me. "Okay, let me change that, carry her to my office," Shawn said.

"Yeah Shawn," Bryce answered as he picked me up.

"Ouch," I moaned.

"Sorry, didn't mean to hurt you," Bryce apologized as he walked out of the door carrying me. I could hear Shawn screaming at AJ and I was glad. She deserved it.

"It's all right, it's not your fault," I said. He walked slowly to Shawn's office so not to hurt me.

"Okay here you are?" Bryce said as he put me down gently on the couch. Then he pulled a chair over towards me.

"Thanks, for pulling AJ off of me."

"Well, I wasn't exactly going to leave her on you. Did you actually go after her?" Bryce asked.

"Surprisingly, no I didn't, just the opposite happened."

"Why did she?" I told the Bryce the whole story, and when I was finished he was smiling and laughing. As we were joking about it Shawn came into his office.

"What's so funny?" Shawn asked.

"Oh God Shawn, you have to hear why AJ went after Candy," Bryce said.

"Okay now that I am hearing two different stories explain yours."

"What? She is saying that I went after her?" I questioned even though I knew the answer.

"Yeah she is."

"Oh yeah that's why I was on the floor. You don't believe her right?" I asked.

"You told me that if she said anything to you, you'd hit her," Shawn said and I couldn't believe what I was hearing, he actually believed her, "But I don't believe that you would do something like that."

"Oh thank God. Someone around here actually believes me," I said relieved.

"Even though I believe you, I want to hear the real story," Shawn told me.

"Okay sure, well AJ started to brag about her getting Bryce and me apart. She was saying how she purposely had us sent to you, because you would split us up. But anyway she was saying how, ever since her and Bryce met, there was something between them. So I said 'I bet Bryce did think there should be something between them' and then when she started to smile and nod I added 'Yeah like a continent.' Then she jumped at me," I said and Shawn was laughing right along with Bryce.

"See isn't it funny?" Bryce asked.

"I have to admit it is," He answered patting me on the shoulder.

"Ouch!" I screamed.

"I am so sorry I forgot about that, let me call the doctor and Bryce go get her an ice pack," He ordered picking up the phone. After Shawn put down the phone Bryce came back in.

"Here you are," He said handing me the ice pack.

"Guys I want to apologize to you both. I should have known that, no matter what I did AJ would have acted up. I know now I should never have told you two not to see each other. You two can see each other, but please don't go bragging to AJ about this. Also Candy, we have this solution around here where if there are two students fighting they are put into a cabin, called the cabin of isolation. It is where the two students have to stay in there together till they work their problems out. I want you and AJ to go there, I know you hate this, but we can't have you two fighting for the next four years while you're here. Kim or I will come four times a day to bring your three meals and a snack at night. Please do this for me, I want you and AJ to go there and work out your problem with each other, okay?" Shawn told me.

"Alright, but for how long will we be there?" I asked.

"As long as it takes you two to work this out."

"In other words we will be there for a long time huh?"

"Maybe so. I'll take you and AJ there tomorrow, if the doctor says you can get out of bed," Shawn told me.

The doctor came in and told me that my headache was nothing really, it just hurt from me hitting it on the floor. Also she told me to keep my arm in a sling for a week and not to use it a lot. Unfortunately, she didn't say I had to stay in bed.

"Candy, you have to go to bed now, same with you Bryce," Shawn told us.

"What about AJ? I mean is she going to be in the same room with me? I really don't think that would be a good idea," I asked.

"Don't worry about AJ, Kim is having AJ in her room for tonight," Shawn explained, "I will be coming to get you tomorrow morning, and be careful with your arm tonight. Goodnight Candy, Bryce."

"Night Shawn," Both Bryce and I said.

"So you and AJ get to spend time together alone, for a long time, how fun that is for you," Bryce joked.

"Yeah fun fun, I just can't wait."

Bryce walked me back to my cabin, and when we got there he gave me a kiss goodnight. I couldn't believe it, we were just standing there and I was just about to say goodnight and he just all of a sudden kissed me on the lips. When I walked into the cabin, I had the biggest smile on my face. I couldn't believe how good a kisser he was. That was the best kiss I had ever had, and I have kissed a lot of guys. I fell asleep thinking about him.

Chapter 4

I was awoken at 7am, by Shawn saying to get my clothes packed and then to go to his office.

"Shawn I just unpacked my clothes and stuff and it is also way too early. Can I please just have another hour of sleep?" I begged.

"Sorry, but no. Also hurry up," He said. I crawled out of bed and got all my stuff together. When I was ready I grabbed my bag and started to Shawn's office.

"Hi," Bryce said as he ran up behind me and put his arms around my waist.

"Oh hi, Bryce," I said as I turned around and gave him a soft kiss on the cheek.

"Try and work everything out with AJ as soon as possible, so I can see you. I'll try and sneak in a few times," He said making me smile. I never realized that I wasn't going to be able to see Bryce while I was in there.

"I'll try, but it will be hard. Well I got to go and start my adventure with AJ."

"Hey hold on a minute," Bryce said.

"Yeah?" I asked turned to him.

"I have never met a girl like you. You are just so sweet, funny, and perfect. I was wondering if you would be my girlfriend?" He said pulling out a ring with two hands holding a heart, and a crown on top of it. I just jumped to him wrapping my good arm around his neck, hugging him so tightly. "So that's a yes right?"

"Of course that's a yes," I said giving him a huge kiss. I could hear Austin and Hobie cheering behind us. I looked over to them laughing. This was the best moment of my life and I didn't want it to end, unfortunately while Bryce was giving me another kiss Shawn, Kim, and AJ walked over.

"Umm…Candy you have to leave," Shawn said.

"Here you are," Bryce said putting the ring on my right ring finger.

"I'll see you soon," I said and Bryce gave me a kiss on the cheek before I followed Shawn.

"Here you two are. I'll bring you breakfast at 8:30," Shawn said to AJ and me. The cabin was the ugliest thing I have ever seen in my life. It was dark, cold, smelly, and just plain ugly. It had this misty and molding feeling to it.

"So why were you and Bryce so lovey-dovey?" AJ asked with an attitude right after Shawn left.

"Don't worry about it; I don't to get in another fight with you. I don't want or need another arm hurt," I said looking down at my arm in the sling, which surprisingly didn't really hurt.

"If it is any consolation I didn't mean to hurt it," AJ said and I think she agreed with me to not fight.

"It's okay, it doesn't really hurt that much, but don't tell Shawn I'm doing this," I said as I took my arm out of the sling.

"Fine."

AJ and I stayed at the cabin for three days so far, and we never talked. Shawn tried to make us talk many of times, but we still didn't. I wasn't going to talk to unless she did first. After the fourth day, I couldn't stand it, I was sick of staying there, and I missed Bryce so much, that I just couldn't keep my mouth shut for another minute.

"AJ, can we make a truce, cause I really don't want to stay here any longer?" I asked.

"What kind of truce?" AJ asked.

"If I don't fight with you, you leave me alone," I said.

"What about Bryce?" AJ asked.

"Do you really think he likes you?" I asked, "Be truthful."

"No I know he doesn't, but since the day I saw him I wanted him; I'm used to getting what I want. But then when I saw how he was with you, I knew he never was going to be mine. So I started taking Bryce not liking me out on you," AJ exclaimed. We were silent for about 5 minutes.

"So do we have a truce, even with Bryce?" I asked.

"Yeah."

"Good because of two reasons, one I am Bryce's girlfriend, and I also I am starting to hate the smell of this cabin, it is starting to make me sick," I said making AJ laugh.

"Come on let's go and tell Shawn," She said to me.

"Yeah," I agreed.

We walked into Shawn's office and he looked so surprised to see us.

"Well I'll be," Shawn said. "So you two have worked out everything?" AJ and I looked at each other and then said at the same time,

"Yep."

"You aren't just saying that to get away from each other?"

"Shawn, don't you think we would have done that sooner?" I said wondering why we didn't do that before.

"Why didn't you?" Shawn asked.

"I guess each of us were just too proud to even talk to each other, but Candy made the first move," AJ said giving me all the credit.

"Well, AJ did agree on the truce, so it wasn't just me," I said smiling at her.

"Okay you two have proved me wrong, I thought you'd be there for at least year. You can go back to living in your own cabin."

"Okay thanks, Shawn," We both said and went running out of his office.

"I have to go and see Bryce before I die," I said running in the opposite direction of AJ.

"Okay c-ya later, Candy," AJ called to me as I waved to her. I went running into Bryce's cabin.

"Hey Austin, where is Bryce?" I asked.

"Oh hi Candy, I think he took a walk to the lake. He has been missing you a lot," Austin said.

"Thanks Austin, see you around," I said running out of the cabin.

"Hey Candy, you got out?" Angel said.

"Yeah, but I'll talk to you later, I am going to see Bryce," I said almost running her over. I went running to the lake and I saw Bryce sitting on the bank there. I decided I was going to surprise him. I went walking slowly and quietly over to him. I slowly gave him a kiss on the cheek and put my arms around his neck.

"Candy!" He said as he jumped a little, "You got out."

"Yeah, AJ and I have a truce," I said.

"Oh I can't believe it."

"Which that I am here or that AJ and I made a truce?"

"Both," He said giving me the biggest, most comforting hug ever. "I know it was only 4 days, but I missed you."

"I missed you too," We spent an hour laying in the grass. I was laying on Bryce's chest with his arm around me. I never felt this good in all my life; even when I was with Joel.

"What are you two doing?" Kim said making me jump.

"What aren't we allowed to spend time together?" Bryce asked with an attitude.

"I don't think Shawn would approve of this."

"I don't think Shawn would care," I said.

"Don't get an attitude with me. Also aren't you supposed to be in the cabin of isolation?"

"No she isn't, I just let her and AJ out of there when they came to see me telling me that they worked out their problems," Shawn said.

"Okay, but what do you think of them being together alone?" Kim asked.

"Just let them be, they haven't been able to see each other for longer than an hour or two for awhile. I trust them both." With that saying I couldn't believe it, an adult, a responsible adult actually trusts me. "Also Candy your mom and stepbrother are coming to see you tomorrow."

"What? No!" I yelled.

"What's the problem?" Shawn asked as Kim was walking away from him. I think she was mad at him for going against her.

"Not Clint, my mom I'll live with, but not him," I begged.

"I can't say to your mom that he isn't allowed to come unless I had a good reason," Shawn said.

"Shawn can I talk to you?" I asked.

"Yeah of course," He said sitting down next to Bryce and me.

"Actually, I mean alone. Sorry Bryce."

"It's okay don't worry about it," He said giving me a hug.

"Okay, come on Candy we can go to my office," Shawn said leading the way.

Chapter 5

I walked into Shawn's office and I was scared to death, and I think Shawn could tell.

"Is something wrong?" He asked.

"Yes," I said nodding and I just started to cry.

"What's wrong?" He said coming to sit next to me on the couch. "What is it?"

"I don't know if I can do it," I said shaking my head.

"You can tell me anything. Is it about your stepbrother on why you don't like him?"

"Yeah," I said crying harder.

"What?" He said in a comforting voice.

"He is really mean to me," I said.

"He doesn't seem like it."

"Well, he didn't seem mean to me at first and he sure doesn't seem that way to my mother. She loves him, even more than she has ever loved me," I said.

"He seems as if he is really fond of you."

"That's the problem!" I burst out.

"Huh?"

"Shawn, Clint is…is…he is really abusive to me," I said crying even harder than before.

"Like how, yelling, hitting, and touching?"

"He...he... I can't."

"You already told me a lot, just tell me the rest."

"Okay, Clint yells, hits, and...and he touches me," I said.

"Really?"

"Yeah I'm sorry, I didn't want him too, but I couldn't tell him no. I tried I really did try. It's my fault that he did this."

"No, no it is not your fault. He has the problem, not you. It is not your fault. If it wasn't you, it would be some other girl. What did he do? I know this is going to be hard, but please I need to know."

"He would come into my room at night, while my mom was out or at work or with one of her boyfriends. He would come in and I would pretend to be sleeping, hoping he would leave me alone. He would flip me over on my back and sit on my stomach, so when he woke me up I wouldn't be able to move. Shawn, please, I don't want to have to relive these memories again. I already wake up in the night from nightmares about them," I begged him to let me stop.

"Okay, you don't have to tell me now, but I am going to have to call child services. I have no choice, but to. And when your mom comes tomorrow I want you to tell her, please. I will get one of the guys take Clint around so he is not here."

"Don't have it be Bryce, I want him here with me."

"Okay," Shawn said. "Do you want to go tell him?"

"I guess I better."

"Okay, do you want to sleep in here tonight, and I'll keep an eye on you?" Shawn asked.

"Umm…no it's okay," I said and I was still crying a little after I went out of his office and back down to the lake. I sat back down next to Bryce.

"Are you okay?" Bryce asked after he saw I was crying.

"Bryce I have to tell you something about my past," I told him.

"Okay, what is it?" I told him all about Clint, from him hitting me and hurting me to the gory details of him touching me. I hated bringing all those dreadful memories, which led me to drugs, up. I also felt relieved at the same time to have someone else know about it.

I could almost see the memories as if they were being acted for me on stage. Bryce kept quiet through the whole thing, and I just couldn't bear to look into his eyes, so I just kept my eyes on the ground while telling him. I knew it wasn't my fault all this happened, but it just felt like there must have been something for me to do. I had a feeling of hatred towards myself, because of all the things I let Clint do to me. I was so afraid that Bryce was going to be mad at me for what happened, I didn't want him to hate me. When I finished telling my story I looked up at Bryce, and he wasn't at all mad, he actually looked sad as if he was about to cry.

"So that is why you started using drugs huh?" He asked.

"Yeah," I answered.

"I am so sorry, but can I kill Clint when he comes tomorrow?" He said and I knew he wasn't joking.

"No I want you with me when I tell my mother this, Shawn is asking me tell her and also child services whenever they come," I told him. "You're not mad at me though?" I asked.

"No I'm not, why would I be?"

"I don't know, I just thought you would be."

"I'm not mad at all at you. It isn't your fault that Clint has a huge problem, which I may be solving for him tomorrow."

"Don't cause a problem with him, please. I want to do that to him," I said as I saw Shawn walk out of the trees.

"Bryce, you have a class right now. Candy, you will be starting classes the day after tomorrow," Shawn said.

"Okay, Shawn. I'll see you later tonight at dinner," Bryce said to me giving me a kiss on the cheek.

"Bye Bryce," I said.

"So did he take it okay?" Shawn asked.

"Yeah other than that he wants to kill Clint now, but I told him not to cause trouble with Clint. Shawn, I am afraid my mom won't believe me, when I tell her."

"She may not, but we can only hope. The people from child services will be here the day you start classes, so you'll be missing a few."

"What will they do to me, and to Clint?" I asked.

"Well, they will most likely question both you and Clint. You may also have to go to court," When I groaned Shawn noticed how upset I was about that, "I'll be there with you every step of the way. Also if they find Clint guilty he will most likely be put in jail for it, or in some place where he could get help, so he stops that," Shawn explained.

"What about me?" I asked.

"Well, you will probably stay here for your four years, like you were before, unless your mother has something against you staying here."

"Okay so I'll be staying here, cause after my mom hears this she isn't going to want me home, and I also won't want to go home. Home has too many memories for me. I wouldn't be able to handle it," I told him.

"Okay, but you'll never know what is going to happen, till it does," Shawn said.

"Yeah I know, well since probably everyone in my cabin is in class I am going to go relax," I said getting up off the grass.

"Okay, do you want me to send Bryce there when he is done with his classes?" Shawn asked.

"Umm...if he wants to come you can tell him to," I said walking away towards my cabin.

When I walked in, it was just like I thought everyone was at their classes. I saw that AJ brought my bag back from the cabin of isolation. I knew that no one would be walking in here for a while so I decided that I would write in my diary. When I went to pull it out I remembered my cigarettes I pulled them out and took a long look at them, and I knew I couldn't smoke them. Shawn and all these people are trying everything to help me and I figured I would throw them away as a thank you to them. I tossed them in the garbage can next to my bed. I couldn't believe I just did that. There wasn't any part in my mind that would have believed I did that. But I was glad I did. I pulled my diary out and opened it up and started writing-

Dear Diary,
The day I have been dreading is coming tomorrow. I told Shawn about Clint (S/B), I told Shawn about him hitting me, touching me and all that stuff. But tomorrow I am confronting my mom and telling her, and then the day after tomorrow I have to tell child services about it. I am so afraid that none of them will believe me. Do you think they will?

I don't, I have to admit that. I am surprised that Shawn did. I also told Bryce and I am glad he believed me, I care about him so much. I asked him if he could stay with me while I tell my mom and child services and he agreed to. He now wants to kill Clint for doing all that stuff to me.

Guess what? Bryce asked me to be his girlfriend, isn't it great? I think it is the best thing that happened to me. Well I got to go, I'll tell you what happens with child services and my mother.

Luv ya,

Candy

I set down my diary and just laid on my bed staring at the ceiling. All of a sudden I just started to cry. It just hit me that I will have to persuade my mom to believe me, and I knew she wasn't going to. She cares about Clint so much more than she could ever care for me. I actually miss my mom a little. Even though we always fought with each other, I did care about her and I did care about what she thinks of me. I brushed the tears out of my eyes thinking that I should wait to cry after I found out what my mom says. I really was worried about what was going to happen to me after child services found out about this. While I was thinking to myself I heard a knock on the door.

"Come in," I said making sure I didn't look as if I was crying.

"Hey Candy. Is Angel in here, we are going to the same class and she told me come here and wait for her?" Hobie said to me.

"No she isn't here yet, but make yourself comfortable while you wait," I said.

"Okay," He said sitting on Angel's bed. "So when do you start classes?" He asked.

"The day after tomorrow, but I will be missing some of them," I said.

"Why?"

"Shawn is having me talk to someone on that day," I said, I didn't want to explain who or why.

"Oh okay, I wish I could get out of some classes. This is even worse than my old school," He said.

"If you don't mind me asking, why are you here?"

A. M. Lahrs

"Well, I got in fights a lot, and I was skipping school to do drugs with a couple of friends."

"Oh okay," I said and just then Angel walked in.

"Hey Angel," Hobie said.

"Hi Candy, hi Hobie.   Are you ready to go?" She asked.

"Yeah," He answered.

"Candy, Bryce wanted me to tell you that he'll be right over he just has to put his books in his room. He doesn't have anymore classes today," Angel said.

"Oh okay, thanks Angel," I said as she was walking out the door with Hobie.

"Bye Candy," Hobie called as he closed the door.

After about 5 minutes I was so bored waiting for Bryce to come that I fell asleep.

"Candy," I heard someone say. I woke up to Kaye walking over to me and Bryce was sitting right next to me.

"How long have two been here?" I asked Bryce.

"I have been here for about three hours and Kaye just got here," Bryce answered.

"Why didn't you wake me?"

"You just looked so sweet there, so I didn't want to wake you."

"But you do have to get up now, it is dinner and Shawn will get mad at you if you miss it," Kaye said.

"Okay," I answered. Bryce, Angel, Kaye, and I walked to the cafeteria together, and we got a table with AJ and the guys in our group.

"So AJ, you and Candy get along now?" Kaye asked.

"Yeah, we are," AJ answered with me nodding.

"Umm...what is this supposed to be?" I asked pointing at the food.

"I think it is roast beef with cooked vegetables and that's a salad and the thing next to the salad is...is...honestly I don't know what the hell it is," Jay was saying.

"Watch you language, Jay," Kim said.

"Sorry, Kim."

"What in God's name is this?" I asked.

"That would be pudding," Kim answered.

"Eww, gross. It sure doesn't look like it," I said as she walked away, "Okay all I am eating off this plate is the salad. I don't eat anything that I can't figure out what it is," I said.

"No Candy, you will eat everything off this plate," Shawn said from behind me.

"But come on Shawn, it's not my fault I don't like this food."

"Well pretend you do. I want you to eat something," Shawn said.

"Then give me something I like. I am very picky about food. If I only like the thing a little bit, I won't eat it."

"Fine as long as you eat everything tomorrow," He gave in.

"Okay I will," I said. After Bryce and I were done eating we went for a walk in the forest, but Kim told us we had to be back in a half-hour. If we weren't she was going to send a search party out to find us.

"Are you nervous about talking to your mom tomorrow?" Bryce asked as he went to hold my hand.

"Terrified, but I am glad that Shawn is letting you to get out of classes to be with me," I said.

"Me too."

"You probably won't like what I am going to say, but I want Clint in there while I tell my mom. I want to hear what he has to say about it. I also have a plan on how I can get my mom to believe me. I am going to tell her only about him touching me, and I figure he will get mad and maybe hit me or grab my arm or something like that. Then if he does I can say he also did that to me."

"It is a good plan, but if he does do that I'm going after him."

"Bryce," I said.

"Okay maybe I won't, but then maybe I will. I'll decide the moment it happens." After awhile of walking around hand in hand Bryce walked me back to my cabin.

"I'll see you tomorrow and don't worry about it. It will be all okay," Bryce said to me, and then he gave me one of the greatest kisses I have ever had in my life. And he has a lot to try to top, since I have kissed so many guys.

"Night Bryce," I said.

"Night Candy, and remember just get some sleep and don't worry about tomorrow."

"I won't," I lied. I walked into my cabin and Kaye was sitting there reading a book.

"Hi Kaye, where is everyone?"

"They all are taking a walk."

"Oh, why didn't you go?" I asked.

"I didn't feel like it; are you like trying to get rid of me or something?"

"No it's not that, I was just wondering," I said.

"Is there something wrong, you look bothered?" Kaye asked.

"Yeah actually there is, but I don't want to talk about it," I answered.

"Okay, but if you ever need someone to talk to I'm always here."

"Thanks; each day you remind me more and more like Joel."

"I'll take that as a complement."

"It is," I said as AJ, May, and Angel walked in laughing.

"What's so funny?" Kaye asked.

"We just caught Kim and Shawn kissing each other," Angel said. That surprised me. I never thought of Kim and Shawn as anything other than colleagues.

"And then they saw us and they gave us this whole long lecture on why we shouldn't be doing what they were," AJ said.

"I guess we had to be there," Kaye said just as Kim walked in.

"Girls, you have to get some sleep now. And AJ, May, and Angel, remember what we talked to you about," Kim said and then left. And right after she closed the door Angel,

May, and AJ just broke out laughing. After they stopped laughing and I finished reading the 4th chapter in the book I was reading I fell asleep worrying about tomorrow.

Chapter 6

The next morning when I woke up it was only 5:30am and everyone else was asleep. I went into the bathroom to take a shower and everything. When I got out it was still only 6am and I knew everyone else wouldn't be up till 7:30am, but I decided that I would go into Shawn's office and sit there waiting till he got up. I walked into his office and he was sitting there in his chair.

"Hi Shawn, I didn't realize you were in here, if I did I would have knocked."

"It's okay," He said just as I was turning around to leave "Come in here and sit down. Why are you up so early?"

"I just woke up, I guess I am nervous about today and tomorrow. What about you?"

"I had some work to do before everyone else got up."

"Anything I can help you with?" I asked.

"Umm…actually yes are you good with math?" Shawn asked.

"I'm all right at it, I'm no mathematician, but I can add, subtract, multiply, and divide."

"Well that will be good enough. Okay this is what I want you to do, on the bottom of each one of these pages there is a total amount of money typed on there, in front of the money there is a plus sign or a minus sign. The plus sign means that I gained money, but the minus means I lost money. If you can count it all up and find out if I lost or gained money and how much. Can you figure that all out?" Shawn explained.

"Yeah, that doesn't sound too hard," I answered him as he handing me about twenty papers. "Hey Shawn what time did my mom say she was coming?"

"She said at about 8:30-9 o'clock."

"Alright, did I tell you that I want Clint to stay in the room while I am telling my mother?"

"No you didn't, but why?"

"I want to know what he is going to say to my mother after he hears this, and if he wasn't there I wouldn't know. Also I finished adding it up, if I am correct you lost $1,230.58."

"Oh jeez that's not good. And I understand about the Clint thing. If you want you can get Bryce up and the two of you can eat breakfast now, since you'll be missing it while you are talking to your mom," Shawn said looking down at the papers that I handed back to him.

"It's okay if I go into his room?"

"Yeah just try not to wake the other guys up," Shawn told me.

"Alright," I said walking out of his office. I walked across the lawn over to the guy's room. And while I was walking I noticed how peaceful and beautiful it was in the morning. Being sober does have its advantages you notice things clearly. I crept quietly into Bryce's room and saw him sleeping in the bed farthest from the door. When I walked over to him I hated to wake him up, he just looked so cute lying there.

"Bryce," I whispered, shaking him. "Bryce," I said a tad bit louder.

"Hmm," He groaned.

"Bryce, it's me Candy."

"Candy," He said more awake.

"Yeah, sorry to wake you up, but Shawn said that I could get you so we could eat breakfast."

"It's okay, stay right here and let me get ready," He whispered as he was walking into his bathroom leaving me sitting on his bed. About 10 minutes later he walked out of the bathroom looking cute as ever. "Come on let's go before we wake the other guys up," Bryce said putting his arm over my shoulders, leading me out of his room.

"I want to thank you again for agreeing to stay with me," I said.

"It's all right, I would do anything for you."

"Thank you," I said putting my hand in his. He looked down at me and smiled. It was the kind of smile that made me gush. We walked into the cafeteria and Shawn was sitting down in there drinking a coffee.

"Morning Shawn," Bryce said sitting down. "Shawn why did you tell us that we weren't allowed to drink coffee when you are now?"

"Because Bryce when I told you that you couldn't I didn't have any decaffeinated coffee, but we just got some yesterday," Shawn answered.

"Why weren't they be able to have coffee anyway?" I asked.

"Because caffeine is a drug," Shawn told me.

"Really?" I asked surprised and Shawn nodded. After we ate breakfast the three of us went to Shawn's office and Kim was sitting there.

"Hi Kim," Shawn said.

"Hi where were you, and why are they up so early?"

"We were eating breakfast and they are up early because they have something to do around 8:30 so they would be missing breakfast if they didn't eat now," Shawn told her.

"Am I going to get clued in on this?" Kim asked; Shawn looked back at me as I was shaking my head.

"I can't tell you Kim; it would be Candy's business to tell you not mine," Shawn explained.

"Fine, but it is unlike you to keep something from me," Kim said.

"If I need to tell someone I swear you will be the one I tell," Shawn said.

"You better not have to tell," I said giving Kim a mean look.

"I guess I should leave you three alone," Kim said walking out the door.

"Yeah and if she didn't leave then I was going to tell her that she had to leave," I said.

"Come on Candy give her a break. Not many of the kids here go to her or tell her things, they always come to me. So she doesn't know a lot of the things that I do. I try to tell her things, but a lot of times the kids that talk to me don't want anyone else to know. She really wants kids to ask her for help especially the girls and at times I rather have the girls ask her about their problems, because I know she would be able to help them better. There are only two girls who ask her about things and they are AJ and May," Shawn explained.

"Is that why she favors AJ so much?" I asked.

"What do you mean?"

"Didn't you notice that when Kim sent Bryce and me here to get punished because of AJ and you told Kim to go talk to her, AJ never got punished," I told him.

"No I didn't realize that I thought Kim did punish her."

"No Candy's right, AJ was never punished for anything," Bryce said.

"If I realized that, that had happened I would have punished AJ, but that never was called to my attention," Shawn said.

"Shawn what time is it?" I asked.

"It is 8:25, if you want you can go out and wait for your mom," Shawn told me.

"Okay, I guess I will; Bryce do you want to come?"

"I'll meet you out there, I need to talk to Shawn for a second," Bryce exclaimed.

"Alright I'll see you in a bit," I said and left the room. I walked out side and everyone else was awake and wandering around the campus.

"Hi Candy," Someone said from behind me, and I turned around to see who it was, but it was a guy I have never seen before.

"Hi," I said.

"How are you doing here?" He asked.

"I'm doing all right, this may seem rude, but who are you?"

"Oh I am stupid, I forgot you only know a few people around here, but anyway I am Zeke. Not to brag or anything, but I am one of the more popular guys around this place," He told me.

"Okay, well hi then. And I see that you already know me."

"Yeah a lot of the guys around here have been talking about you and I just had to meet you."

"Oh okay," I said wondering why people have been talking about me.

"I heard you also have got in some trouble with AJ and were sent to the cabin of isolation."

"Yeah we were there, but we worked out our problem." It made me uncomfortable that some guy I just met has heard of me and knows things about me. I didn't even like people I know hearing things about me, let alone someone I saw for the first time.

"I was there before with this one guy and after a week we couldn't stand each other anymore that we lied to Shawn and told him we worked everything out, but we never did and we still hate each other," Zeke told me.

"I don't know why I didn't do that. I guess neither one of us thought about that."

"What are you doing here Zeke?" I heard Bryce's voice from behind me.

"Hello Bryce. I was just talking to this lovely girl here," Zeke said giving an evil smile to Bryce.

"I think you should leave, Zeke," Bryce said coldly.

"I don't," Zeke commented.

"Leave now or I'll kick your ass like I did before," Bryce declared. I have never heard

Bryce sound that mean. He didn't seem like the type of person who would ever get mad.

"Fine I'll leave, but not because I am afraid to fight you again, it's just I don't want to have to be in a cabin with you again."

"I'm sure you're not afraid," Bryce said sarcastically as Zeke walked away.

"What was up with that?" I asked.

"Zeke and I *hate* each other."

"Why?"

"Because when Angel was my girlfriend, he tried to get her in bed with him. She told him no because of me and he started with me, and I just fought right back," Bryce explained.

"Did you win?" I asked smiling.

"I guess you could say that; I gave him a sore arm for a week, a black eye, a bloody nose, and a *really* bad head-ache."

"What about you?" I asked.

"He just gave me a sore cheek for about an hour, and he hates me even more for that," Bryce said laughing.

"Well I am glad you won, cause I don't like him either. He is too…well untrustworthy. He actually reminds me of Clint, and trust me when I saw that I am never going to like anyone who reminds me the slightest bit of Clint," I said.

"Well, that makes me extremely happy," After about five minutes of talking with Bryce I saw my mothers car pull up the street.

"Oh God, it's her. I don't think I can do this," I said shaking my head almost getting up to leave.

"Yes you can, and I am right here by you," Bryce reassured me. I got up off of the step that I was sitting on, with Bryce holding my hand tightly. My mom stepped out of the car with Clint right beside her. I felt hatred toward him and I wished he was never brought into my life. I saw that he was looking mad at Bryce holding my hand.

"Hello Candace," My mother said and I could tell she was mad at me for the last visit we had.

"Hi mom," I said quietly and I felt like I was going to burst out crying.

"Candy, I'll go get Shawn, okay?" Bryce said to me and gave me a hug as I was nodding.

"Who does he think he is hugging you like that?" Clint asked so coldly that it scared me.

"He's my boyfriend."

111

"He only likes you because of one reason," Clint said.

"That's not true, he isn't like some people I know," I answered.

"Hello, Mrs. Walkinson, Clint," Shawn said shaking each of their hands.

"Hello again Shawn. Has Candy been getting in trouble?" My mother asked.

"No but, Candy has told me something very important and I think she should tell you. So if you and your son would come to my office Candy would like to tell it to you," Shawn said.

"Okay, come on Clint," My mom said and we started walking to Shawn's office.

"Would you two please have a seat?" Shawn said pointing to two chairs sitting in front of his desk. My heart was beating faster and faster as they sat down.

"What is it Candace? And this better be important," My mom said.

"You...you are just a horrible person. Anything your daughter has to say should be important to you," Bryce yelled from where he was standing in front of the door.

"Don't tell her how to raise her child, boy," Clint yelled back.

"Well somebody ought to, if she thinks that way, she shouldn't even be a parent!" Bryce yelled louder.

"Bryce, please," I said.

"I'm sorry Candy," Bryce apologized and walked over to me.

"Okay, Candy I think you should tell your mom now, before another argument breaks out," Shawn said.

"Mom there is a reason why I did drugs, ran away, and everything else I have done. In a way I shouldn't be saying that, because they were my mistakes not the other person's. I do need to tell you something that I have been hiding from you for awhile, and I didn't tell you before because I was afraid and because the person that it has to deal with, you know. The sad thing is I have you here and yet I still don't want to tell you, but I don't think I have a choice in the matter. Mom, Clint isn't the kind of person you think he is."

"What do you mean?" My mom asked.

"Yeah what do you mean?" Clint said as if you he didn't know.

"You shut up right now; you know what I mean. I don't want to hear a word out of your mouth till I am finished," I said coldly. "Mom, what I mean is, that Clint is not the sweet boy you thought he was."

"How so?" My mom questioned.

"Mom, I'm sorry it is my fault," I said breaking out into tears.

"Candy, that is not true, you know none of it was your fault," Shawn spoke up.

"What happened?" My mom asked looking sort of sad.

"Clint…Clint he abused me mom."

"What? No mom, she's lying!" Clint yelled.

"Mom he hit me, pushed me, slapped me in the face and then in the mornings while you were at work and at night he would come into me room, and he would…he would touch me and have sex with me!" I cried out over Clint lying to my mom.

"Mom, she is lying, why would I ever like a slutty, skank like her?" Clint said to my mom.

"Drop dead ass hole!" Bryce yelled. "You are the biggest lying prick that has ever walked on the face and this planet, and you deserve to go to hell!"

"Mom, they all are lying. And Candy, I cared for you, I helped you out, and this is how you repay me," Clint said walking right up to me.

"Helped me, cared for me, yeah right. You and your dumb ass father walked into my life and both of you just kill ever ounce of good in me. I wish you hadn't set foot in my house. My life would have been better and my mother's life would have been a lot easier if you never showed up. I wouldn't be here and my mom wouldn't hate me now. How I feel about you now is that I wish you would walk right out of this door and head for the nearest cliff and I would be the one person at your funeral laughing. Your dad left my life, why can't you do the same? Also don't call my mom your mom, she isn't. If I remember correctly your mother is the one who walked out on you and your father, and I applaud her," I screamed.

"You bitch!" Clint yelled raising his arm to hit me, but put it back down.

"Hit me, you've done it before, why won't you just do it again? Oh wait I know why, you don't want my mom to think it is actually true do you? That wonderful, great Clint would ever hit a girl, especially his stepsister. I swear I want my mother to believe me, but if she won't, child services will when they come here tomorrow to talk to me, about you and your disgusting habits."

"Wait Candy, I think you're going a little overboard; I don't think child services would be the answer. They could take Clint away, and that wouldn't be right," My mom said calmly.

"But abusing me is okay, right?" I said looking at her in amazement.

"I didn't say that, but I'm not sure I can believe you, it is just you have lied millions of times, how do I know that you're not lying now? I don't think I can believe you, and that is not an easy thing for me to say."

"It sure seemed easy," I said to my mom and started crying.

"Shawn, may I ask you something?" Clint asked.

"Yes you may," Shawn answered.

"You don't actually believe her do you?"

"Actually, yes I do believe her. I don't have a doubt in my mind that you did all this to her."

"But she is always lying and this is one of those times," Clint said.

"She has never lied to me, so I wouldn't ever call her a liar, also I know you did this."

"How would you know?" Clint asked.

"Because I can see it in your eyes. I know when a person lies and this is one of those times. I also can see fear in her eyes. If this was untrue she wouldn't be afraid," Shawn said pointing at me.

"Well you are wrong this time," My mom spoke up, "Clint wouldn't ever do something like that. He adored Candy, he cared for her, and I know he isn't like that," My mother said.

"Leave mom, if you can't even try to believe me then just go. Also Clint I want you to know something, I have a person who saw you hurting me before. I won't say who it is, because I don't want you giving that person a hard time. But anyway if I need someone as a witness that person will be there," I said as Clint and my mother were walking out the door.

"Well, you told her," Shawn said.

"Hold on, I'll be right back," I said as I was running out of the door after my mom. "Mom wait!" I yelled as she started getting into her car.

"What is it?" She asked and I could see that she was extremely mad at me.

"Mom, I know you don't believe me and I wish you did, but I want you to know I am sorry for all the trouble I caused you. And I know I have lied to you a lot, but I am not lying now. I would never lie about something like this. I'm not mad at you for not believing me, but I am mad at you for caring about a step-son more than your own flesh and blood daughter," I said.

"I can't believe you on this, it would be easier if I could, but I can't. I know Clint and he wouldn't be like that," My mom said and drove away. I was left standing there wondering why my mother couldn't just trust me this one time.

"I'm proud of you kid," Shawn said from behind me.

"I'm not," I responded.

"Why not? You had the guts to tell your mother your biggest secret ever, and it makes me so proud of you."

"But she didn't believe me and she hates me even more than before. So to me I didn't succeed in this."

"You have way too high standards of yourself, which makes me wonder why you let yourself turn to drugs."

"I don't have high standards of what I do, I have high standards of how well I do them. Why else would you think that Brent would come to see me and want more of what I gave to him before?"

"Okay never mind you don't have to go into detail about Brent," Shawn said.

"Alright, but do you understand what I meant?"

"Yeah, I think I get what you mean," Shawn answered.

"Hey Shawn, where did Bryce go?" I asked looking around for him.

"I think he went canoeing."

"Is he mad at me or something?" I asked scared that he was.

"No, it's just, Candy he cares about you so much that he was as mad as you were about your mom not believing you. And anytime Bryce is having his emotions pulling him in many directions he usually goes to the lake to think," Shawn explained.

"Okay well I am glad he isn't mad at me. Do you think he would mind if I went down to the lake to see him?"

"I doubt it," Shawn answered. "But be back in about a half hour for lunch."

"Okay, I will," I said running down the path to the lake. When I got there I saw Bryce paddling around in the canoe; I didn't want to bother him so I just sat down on the grass and watched him. Bryce looked so cute rowing across the lake, but then he also looked like he was thinking seriously about something. I wondered what he was like before he came here; I just couldn't image him ever doing drugs or fighting.

"Oh hi Candy, I didn't realize you were here," Bryce said getting out of the canoe.

"Hi, Shawn told me you were here."

"Okay, well you did it and you got it all over with."

"Yeah and I have to do it all over again tomorrow. I have to tell Child Services about it, and I know you won't be allowed to stay with me."

"Yeah I know Shawn told me that, but it shouldn't be as hard as today was. You don't know the person one and you already let it out all you have to do is repeat what you said to your mom."

"Yeah I know; I just can't wait till this is all over. Hey I got to go talk to Shawn," I said to Bryce as I jumped up and went on a full sprint to Shawn's office.

"Hey Kim is Shawn here?" I asked.

"No he just went for a little hike, is there anything I can help you with?"

"Do you know where he went hiking to?" I asked.

"He just went left to Cobble Hill Path from there I don't know where he will go," Kim answered.

"Okay I'll be back sometime, I have to talk to him about something important, bye Kim and thanks a bunch."

"Wait Candy, you can't go alone."

"Watch me," I said running down the path to reach Cobble Hill or Shawn which ever came first. I was so out of breath I haven't run in a while, except when I was running away from the two guys who were going to bring me here, but I didn't really count that as running. I ran all the way to Cobble Hill Path and there was no Shawn, but I did see footprints going straight down Cobble Hill Path, so I decided I should follow them.

"Shawn!" I yelled hoping he wasn't that far away, but I got no answer. I went down the path, and just my luck Shawn picked one of the rocky paths that you almost had to climb down it. I was walking not paying that much attention when I looked down and saw I was standing next to a cliff and the footprints went right off of it. I looked down and saw Shawn climbing down the cliff.

"Shawn!" I yelled as loud as I could. "Shawn! Shawn up here!" I said and he looked up.

"Hang on, I'll be up in a bit!" Shawn called up to me. I heard from a few students that Shawn went rock climbing a lot, but I never thought they were serious. I sat down on a rock that was on the other side of the path, and in front of a forest. About ten minutes later I saw Shawn's hand reach up to the top of the cliff. "Hey, can you give me a hand?" Shawn called.

"Oh yeah sure," I said reaching for his hand helping him get up.

"You're not supposed to leave the school with out someone with you."

"Well, Kim told me where you went and then I left, so she knew I was here. She didn't want me to be here, but too late now."

"So, what are you doing here?"

"I had to talk to you."

"And you had to follow me out here break two rules to talk to me."

"What two rules did I break?" I asked.

"One, when someone tells you not to do something you don't, and two you're not allowed to leave school grounds without someone with you. Also you're not going to want to hear this, but I'll have to give you a punishment for that."

"Oh come on. Do you guys give punishment for everything?"

"Basically."

"Even if I needed to tell you something important and I wanted to tell you it right away, and I'd be getting in trouble for that."

"Well technically...yes."

"That sucks."

"It may, but while we are walking back to the school you can talk me," Shawn said putting his arm around my shoulders leading the way down the path.

"I can't believe I am being punished, but anyway I needed to just talk to you. I was there with Bryce when I just realize that I can't handle all of this."

"Okay?" Shawn asked.

"I can't handle all this pressure and everything else. I haven't had this much pressure put on me ever and I am about ready to burst."

"Kid, it's understandable. You have so many things on your mind, how can you not feel stressed? Just remember you have so many people around here that care about you. Bryce and probably every guy at this school would sit down and listen to your problems," Shawn said making me blush and shake my head. "Don't shake your head you know as well as I do that all the guys here would go out with you if you were to ask them. Plus you have me to talk to," Shawn said and it made me feel so good to be liked for more than people like Brent and Clint liked me for.

"Thanks a bunch Shawn. I swear you must be my guardian angel."

"I figure I am a guardian angel to everyone that comes into this school."

"That's true, but thanks for everything, for helping me, for standing up for me, and mostly for believing me."

"It's not a problem, and I want to thank you for trusting me and telling me the truth, but you're still getting punished for today."

"Come on Shawn, please?"

"No, I don't change the rules for anyone else and I can't change them for you; even though your reason for breaking them wasn't a bad reason."

"Fine, what am I going to have to do?"

"Umm…probably kitchen duty for a week."

"What a week?"

"Yes a week, for every rule you break it is three days of kitchen duty, and you broke two."

"Oh joy, a week of serving food and cleaning dishes."

"Hey, it won't only be you there are a few other people who have to join you, for getting in trouble."

"Well that is a plus, who are they?"

"There is only one that I can really remember his name is Zeke."

"Zeke! Oh come on I don't deserve that much punishment."

"What do you mean? You know Zeke?"

"Unfortunately, yes I do know him. And the first thing he did was hit on me. Please Shawn can't you give him a different job?"

"Sorry I can't."

"Oh great," I said sarcastically. "Wow we're already back at school."

"Yeah that was a quick walk. Oh and before you go someplace, you're punishment starts the day after tomorrow and you serve breakfast and lunch and you do the dishes for all three meals."

"Fine. What about my classes?"

"They start tomorrow, but you'll be missing the morning half for when Child Services guy comes," Shawn walked with me to my room.

"Hi girls," Shawn greeted everyone.

"Hi," Everyone said back to him.

"I'll see you later, Candy, see you girls," Shawn said waving good-bye.

"What was that about?" Angel asked.

"Don't worry about it," I said sitting down on my bed opening up my diary the letter from my mom fell out. I opened it up and started reading:

Dear Candy,

I know you aren't happy with me, and I don't blame you, but I wanted you to get help. And I never could give you the help you needed, plus you wouldn't ever let me help you. This is the only thing I could come up with. There is some news that I wanted to tell you before you left, but there really wasn't anytime to. But anyway Clint's father and I are going to be getting back together and maybe getting married again. I want you to be there for it, so I hope you forgive me soon so you can come home, where you belong. Well I hope to talk to you soon, please hurry and get better soon, I'm going to miss you so.

Love always,

Mom

"Oh no!" I said out loud. "I'll be back," I said to Kaye and Angel while running out the door to Shawn's office again. "Shawn you won't believe how bad my life is," I said to him throwing the letter towards him. While he was reading it I was pacing back and forth in his office.

"Oh boy, boy oh boy. That is not at all good for you."

"You're damn right that isn't good."

"Language."

"Sorry."

"It's okay."

"I can't believe this, how could she. She told me the day she kicked Clint's dad out that she never was going to get with another guy like him. And instead of a guy like him she's getting back with the real thing."

"Is he as bad as Clint?"

"Well, he hasn't ever done anything like Clint does, but he is an asshole. He threatened to kick me out of my house about forty times; he also wanted to ship me away to a boot camp for like seven years."

"Okay he is pretty bad too."

"Yeah like father, like son."

"I don't really know what to tell you, but you shouldn't also be worrying about this too. You already have too many things on your mind."

"It's kind of hard not to think about this. God, I swear if all these things happened to me while I was home, I'd probably kill myself."

"Don't say those things Candy," Shawn said looking worried.

"Don't worry I won't do anything here, you people are around too much for me to do anything."

"You realize with you saying that I will be forced to keep an even closer eye on you."

"Okay, sure, but I didn't mean I was going to do anything," I said.

"You may not have, but it scares me to think that you would even think of doing that at home, and I don't want to take any chances."

"I'm sorry, I didn't mean to worry you, you also have enough to worry about, like paying all that money that I counted up, so you can keep this place."

"How did you know about that?"

"First off on each of those papers it said why you need to pay or why you were getting money, also with that I figured that was the only logical reason."

"You're smart you know that?"

"Not really."

"Yeah you are, but you have to promise me one thing."

"Sure anything."

"Don't go telling people about it, not even Kim."

"Okay, besides why would I even be talking to Kim?"

"Just don't say anything."

"I won't, I swear," I promised. "Shawn, what should I do about my mom and Clint's father?"

"I don't know what to tell you."

"How can you not, you always have the answers?"

"No I don't; I wish I could tell you what to do, but the best thing I can say is, don't worry about it, everything will work out," He said.

"Are you sure?"

"I can't be sure about anything, but I will make sure you'll be okay for always."

"If you ever have kids Shawn, you'll be the best father ever."

"Thank you, and speaking of fathers; what ever happened to your father?"

"My mom doesn't really like to talk about him, but I know he left my mom because she was cheating on him, with Clint's dad. He calls me on my birthday and he sends me gifts on Christmas and my birthday, but that's about all I know of him."

"You've seen him right?"

"Yeah, but not since my mom and him broke up, which was about four years ago. I send him pictures of me every year," I explained.

"Well, do you think he would believe you if you told him what Clint did?"

"I'm not sure, but I know he never liked Clint. He met him once, and the last thing he said to me in person was if Clint ever did anything to me or my mother to tell him," I told Shawn reliving the last memory I had with my dad.

"I think you should tell him."

"I know I should but I don't know his number to call him."

"I'll find it out and call him and ask him if he can come here to see you."

"Thanks a lot Shawn; I wish my mother would have married you instead of Clint's dad."

"That makes me happy to hear that, but I don't think you would have liked me before I quit using drugs. Honestly I probably would have done the same thing Clint did to you. Well, maybe not that bad, but I would have been very mean."

"I don't think you would have, people may change while they are doing drugs, but I think you would have chosen the right thing to do," I told him and he just sat there smiling.

"I am glad you think so highly of me. It is very flattering," Shawn said.

"You dedicate your life to helping teenagers in need. That probably makes you the most caring, generous, special person in the world."

"Thank you," Shawn said with the biggest smile on his face. "Okay now before I start to cry let's go get lunch."

"Okay," I said walking out of Shawn's office to the cafeteria.

"Hey Candy," Bryce called to me.

"Hi, Bryce, hey everyone," I said waving to everyone at the table.

"Hi," Everyone answered back.

"What's up?" Bryce asked me.

"What do you mean?" I asked.

"You just looked a bit stressed."

"Yeah, but I'll tell you later what it is about."

"Alright," He said.

"So, I heard you will be on cooking duty with me for a week; that should be fun, real fun," I heard someone behind me say. I turned

around and saw Zeke standing there getting
ready to sit down next to me.

"You heard right, and I don't think your
allowed to sit here.   You're not a Spruce
Falls."

"So what did you do to get cooking duty?"
He asked.

"I went out of school grounds without
anyone," I answered him.

"Not bad."

"Thanks."

"Hey I want to talk to you later."

"Why later?   You can talk now, Zeke," I
said with an attitude that I haven't had since
the second day I was here.

"I think it would be best later.   Meet me in
the shed at 7 tonight, okay?"

"I wouldn't hold your breath if I was you,"
I said in the same snotty voice as before and I
turned back around.

"What you're not coming?" He asked.

"Ding, ding, ding you are correct," I said.

"Why not?   I am the most popular, good-
looking guy here, hello you would be stupid if
you didn't meet me."

"Boy aren't you a modest one," I said
making everyone at my table laugh.   "I guess I

must be stupid, even though I think I am smart, because I have the greatest boyfriend ever and trust me Zeke it isn't and will never be you."

"Well, who is it then?"

"Bryce," I answered.

"Ha, you're going out with him, come on that is just pathetic."

"It's not as bad as if I was with you, I think I'd just die. You'd make me go insane with how great you think you are."

"Get out of here, Zeke. Obviously no one wants you around," Bryce spoke up.

"And if I don't?" Zeke asked.

"I'll be giving you more aches and pains than I did the first time I fought you," Bryce answered.

"Yeah right."

"Don't try me Zeke cause you know I'll do it," By this time everyone in the cafeteria was looking at our table, so I figured I should stop them.

"Bryce please stop, just leave him be. I don't want you to have to go to the cabin of isolation," I tried persuading him.

"Fine, but only because you say so," Bryce gave in.

"Oh, the little bitch is the boss of you, how sweet," Zeke said and before I could grab hold of Bryce he was jumping off his seat and went charging at Zeke.

"Bryce stop!" I yelled as Shawn came running over pulling Bryce off of Zeke. Kim was holding back Zeke, who had a bloody nose, a red mark around his eyes, and his lip was bleeding.

"You're crazy, you idiot!" Zeke yelled trying to get free of Kim's hold.

"You shouldn't have opened your mouth," Bryce said, who only had a red mark on his cheek.

"Both of you shut up now!" Shawn yelled.

"He started it," Zeke lied.

"No you started it you asshole, you came over to *our* table," Bryce yelled back as he got loose from Shawn's grip and went flying at Zeke again.

"Bryce!" Shawn yelled getting a hold of Bryce again. "Candy; take him to my office while I am yelling at him," Shawn ordered. "And don't let him go!"

"Alright, come on Bryce," I said grabbing his arm.

"Oh what a cute couple," Zeke called sarcastically as Bryce turned around.

"No, come on Bryce," I said holding his arm harder. I took Bryce to Shawn's office and made him settle down.

"I hate him!" Bryce declared.

"So do I, but just ignore him, don't start fighting him. That's what he wants he wants you to get in trouble for something he started," I said.

"You seem like you don't even care what he said about you?" Bryce questioned.

"Coming from him not really; I know he is so much worse than I ever could be and I honestly don't care what he thinks of me," I informed him.

"But he is just so...ouch," Bryce said holding his cheek.

"If I go to get you an ice pack you promise me you will not leave."

"I won't leave," Bryce promised. I left the office and started walking back to the cafeteria to get the ice pack in the freezer there. Shawn was still yelling at Zeke.

"What are you doing back?" Kim asked.

"I came to get an ice pack so Bryce's cheek doesn't swell up," I told her.

"You should be watching him," She yelled at me.

"He doesn't need a babysitter," I said to her walking into the kitchen area. "Excuse me but where is the freezer?" I asked the nearest person.

"Over there," They pointed to my left.

"Thanks," I got the ice pack and walked back into the eating area.

"Candy?" Shawn called.

"Yeah Shawn?" I answered walking over to him.

"Can you please take him to the nurse's office?" He said pointing to Zeke.

"No."

"Come on, please?" Shawn asked again.

"Not a chance, besides he needs more help than the nurse could give him. He has so many unsolvable problems."

"You bitch!" Zeke yelled as I turned away flipping my hair in his face, which probably hurt, since he was bleeding all over. I went back to the office and gave Bryce the ice pack and sat down next to him putting my head on his shoulder.

"I wonder what punishment I will be getting now?" Bryce asked.

"I hope not much," I said. Shawn then walked in and he was not looking happy.

"I'm disappointed in you Bryce," Shawn exclaimed.

"Yeah I know, but just give me my punishment and I'll behave," Bryce said.

"Okay, you are not going to like this in one way. You have kitchen duty with Candy."

"Why wouldn't I like that?" Bryce asked confused.

"Let me finish, Zeke is in there, and if you fight again I'll figure out a worse punishment like making you go to the cabin of isolation alone, no visitors," He told Bryce and then turned to me.

"Oh don't tell me I am going to be getting punishment?" I looked surprised.

"No, I just need you to make sure Bryce doesn't get into another fight."

"Alright, but what is Zeke getting for starting the fight?"

"He isn't allowed to talk to you or Bryce and if he does I told him he is going to have to see a shrink for his fighting and he also has another week of kitchen duty."

"Thank you, no more having to talk to him," I said happily and Bryce seemed to agree with me.

"Your welcome, also Candy Child Services are coming at 7:30 so you shouldn't be missing any classes," Shawn explained.

"Okay that is good."

"Yeah it is, but Candy I need to talk to you alone so Bryce will you please leave us for moment?" Shawn asked and I was quite frightened I thought something bad was about to happen.

"Yeah sure, I'll be right outside waiting for you," Bryce said to me, putting his hand on my shoulder. And then he left.

"Don't look so scared, nothing's wrong," Shawn said knowing that I was petrified.

"Good," I sighed in relief.

"Umm…I have three things to tell you, first during your interview tomorrow do you want me there?"

"Yeah if you don't have anything else to do."

"Nope, my time is all yours. Also they will be taping it, like video camera wise."

"Really?" I said not to happy.

"Yeah they have to have it all recorded. The third thing is that I got in touch with your father he said he wants to see you because he has something to tell you. He'll be here the day after tomorrow."

"Really? He wants to see me? Did you tell him about Clint?"

"Yeah I hope you don't mind."

"No, not at all Shawn, I didn't want to have to tell another person."

"All right you're free to go."

"Okay," I said got up and opened the door and then turned around, "Hey Shawn?"

"Yeah?" He asked.

"Thanks, for everything."

"You're welcome, Candy," He said smiling. I walked out of his office and Bryce was waiting there talking to some guys I don't know, but when he saw me he said good-bye to them and walked over.

"Is everything okay?" He asked.

"Yeah, he just wanted to tell me something about tomorrow and also tell me that they got in touch with my dad and he is coming the day after tomorrow."

"Oh."

"He has to tell me something and I am really hoping that when I get out of here he's taking me and not having my mom take me."

"That would be good," Bryce said. "Hey baby, I hate to say this but I got to go. A couple of friends asked me to go play football with them. If you want you can come and cheer me on or even play if you know how," He offered.

"Yeah I think I may come and join you," I said to him.

"Do you know how to play?"

"Kinda, I can catch a ball, throw a ball, kick a ball, tackle people, and run."

"Okay cool, so maybe I'll see you in a bit, bye girl," He said.

"Bye, Bryce," I said watching him run over to his friends.

Chapter 7

I walked into my room and Kaye was sitting on her bed reading a book.

"Oh sorry if I disturbed you," I apologized.

"No, it's okay, you didn't bother me."

"Alright that's good," I said sitting down on my bed.

"Hey can I ask you something?" Kaye asked.

"Yeah sure, what is it?"

"Well first, I know you don't like talking about your life to any of us, but what has been going on with you recently, like your mom and brother coming, you getting out of classes. Also then you have been talking to Shawn a lot, more than anyone else has ever talked to him," I didn't really want to tell anyone about what has been going on, but it seemed like I could trust Kaye with anything.

"Umm…Oh gosh. Okay Clint is not my brother he's my step-brother, I guess I'll start out with that," I started my story with the day I met Clint till today. She listened through the whole thing, never interrupting me. She kept her eyes on me and ears opened the whole time.

"God, no wonder you don't like talking about your family a lot," She said.

"Yeah, I don't want you telling anyone about this. I don't want it to get out," I pleaded.

"You can trust me. I promise I won't say anything."

"Okay thanks a whole lot."

"Yeah it's alright," Kaye answered.

"Hey, Bryce is playing football with a couple of guys; I told him I may go and join them in playing. You want to come?"

"Oh I really don't."

"Come on it will be great," I interrupted her.

"Alright fine," She gave in.

"Cool, I think I should get changed into something that I don't mine getting dirty," I said.

"Me too," Kaye answered. We both got changed, I was wearing some of my old khakis that I had to squeeze into to get them to fit around my waist, and I had on a long-sleeve baby blue hooded shirt. Kaye was wearing black jeans and a red shirt that said 99% devil and 1% angel. I thought it was a cute shirt, but I guess she didn't since she said she hated that shirt.

"Come on," I said heading to the door with her following me. We got to the area where they were playing football. It was in front of the main building. When Bryce saw me he called timeout and came running over to us, he went to give me a kiss, but I stopped him.

"What?" He asked.

"Your face is all muddy, I am not getting a kiss that tastes like dirt, sorry baby," I said and he smiled.

"You ready to play?" He asked.

"Yeah, but is it okay if Kaye joins us too?" I asked him.

"Sure, if she doesn't mind being on the other team."

"I don't care," Kaye answered.

"Cool, come on girls," Bryce said.

"Otay," I said as he grabbed my hand.

"Hey can you be receiver, you know the person that catches."

"I know what a receiver is Hun. I may be a blonde, but come on give me some credit," I said.

"Oh sorry, I didn't really realize you knew football."

"I know it enough," We started playing and it seemed like all the guys playing were very surprised that I could play. They kept congratulating me, and Bryce kept picking me up and kissing me. I had no complaints, except for the mud on both of us. But hey, I love the guy what can you expect. When we were done playing our team won by a lot. I definitely had to get changed, I was a complete mess.

"Hey girl," I heard someone call and I realized it was Shawn.

"Yeah Shawn?" I ran over to him.

"You're pretty, I mean really, really good," He complimented me.

"Oh thanks, I've hung out with guys forever I had to learn something from them at some point," I said. "Hate to be rude, but I got to go and get changed I look horrible."

"All right kid, see ya later."

"Yeah bye Shawn," I ran to my cabin and Kaye was already there. "Hey Kaye, did you have fun?"

"I have to admit that I really did."

"I knew it," After I got changed there was a knock on the door, I got it and I couldn't believe who I saw standing right before me.

Chapter 8

"Oh my God, Joel what are you doing here?" I asked so surprised and Kaye came out of the bathroom to see what was going on. Joel looked horrible he was so pale, and very thin. I mean he has always been thin, but this was too much. It looked as if he hadn't eaten in years.

"Candy," He said and he almost fell over, but both Kaye and I caught him.

"Kaye go get Shawn, now!" I yelled. I dragged Joel over to my bed and laid him down. In about a minute or so Shawn came running in with Kim, Bryce, and Kaye shortly behind him.

"What happened?" Kim asked.

"Shawn is he alright?" I asked.

"I'm not sure, Kim go call 911," He said calmly. "Someone get a cold wash cloth or something," He ordered. Kaye went running to it. Bryce had his hand on my shoulder as Shawn was checking his pulse. "It just seems like he fainted, he's still got a pulse."

"Oh god," I said out loud.

147

"Candy, maybe you shouldn't be here. Bryce take her to my office," He said as Kim came back in.

"No way am I leaving his side!" I yelled.

"They said that they'd be here a soon as possible, they're pretty busy. They also said to try and wake him up, after he does give him food and water, and make sure he stays awake," Kim told Shawn.

"Thanks Kim, now Candy go to my office I don't want you here," Shawn ordered.

"No!" I yelled.

"Candy; listen to Shawn," Kim said.

"Not a chance am I leaving," Kim reached for my arm. "I swear if you even touch me so help me God I will hit you so hard that you will be the one laying on this bed!" I screamed.

"Candy!" Shawn yelled. "This is not the time to be fighting with anyone. Go to my office now! Bryce take her and make sure she stays there. I don't care if you have to tie her down to keep her there. Do not let her leave."

"All right," Bryce agreed and grabbed hold of my hand. When I pulled away, he grabbed me around my waist, and started carrying me to the door. I was kicking frantically and screaming so loud that people started looking towards me, but I didn't care.

"Put me down!" I yelled continuously. When we got to Shawn's office he put me down on the chair and I booked for the door.

"Candy!" He yelled and grabbed hold of my wrist. "Baby, come on," He said trying to be patient with me.

"I should be with Joel, not here," Bryce ended up having to tie my hands to the arms of the chair. I was trying to get loose, when Kim walked in.

"So you ended up having to tie her down," Kim said to Bryce. He just nodded. "Good," She said.

"Excuse me?" Bryce asked.

"I just mean, finally someone has stopped pitying her and did what we should have done awhile ago," She walked over to me and I kicked her in the shin so hard that she couldn't stand and had to sit in Shawn's seat. "You do that again I will tell Shawn and he would be forced to send you the juvenile center."

"I'd get one good thing out of that. I would never have to see your ugly face again," I said still trying to get loose.

149

"You really have come to be the problem child."

"Only to you, Kim. Shawn hasn't said that I am a problem child."

"Do I look like Shawn?" She asked.

"No you look extremely ugly, Shawn doesn't," I said.

"Bryce can you please leave?" Kim asked.

"Fine, but I am telling Shawn everything you said," Bryce said and left.

"I know you hate me girly and I am not to fond of you, but come on. I am a teacher here and I do try to help."

"What help? Make my life horrible?" I remarked.

"As much as I would love to do that no. I want you to tell me the thing you hate most about me. I am letting all the rules down right now. Talk as bad as you want," She said.

"Gee…there are just so many things wrong with you. But the thing I hate most would have to be the way you think of me."

"Keep going on that, I want to hear what you have to say," She told me.

"Okay, I see the looks you give me when I am hanging on Bryce or holding his hand, or whatever. I like him, I've liked him since the day I saw him and trust me it isn't how I used to like guys. I truly care about him."

"Well that is what I am worried about. With your past history with guys any person would be worried."

"So what you're actually saying is that you don't trust me at all."

"Did I say that?"

"You didn't have to. Kim, I am not brain-dead or clueless. Give me some credit, I know when people don't trust me."

"Fine I'll admit it, you are not the most trustworthy student here."

"I may not be, but I am not going to play games with Bryce or any guy ever again. And I am not going to ruin Bryce's life or mine by doing something stupid," I told her. "My life isn't very great at this moment, and I am not going to make it worse."

"Okay, do you hate me for any other reason?"

"Yeah I do. I can probably think of a lot."

"Name them."

"Really? You sure you have enough time?"

"All the time you need."

"Fine. I hate how you favor everyone else over me. Like the thing with AJ. Bryce and I got punishment from Shawn, and yet AJ didn't get ever get any punishment from you."

"AJ just needed to cool off steam. Her emotions took the better of her. Besides it wasn't like she meant anything by it, she was just a mad."

"So was Bryce when he swore at her."

"But swearing is not allowed here."

"That is amazing. When I got here Shawn explained all the rules to me. And swearing was not one of the rules. He told me there were three rules; no drugs, no fighting, no sex. He never told me I wasn't allowed to swear," I argued.

"Fine you got me there, maybe AJ should have got punished for starting the fight, but that is done and over with," She agreed. "Anything else that you hate about me?"

"Yeah, one minute you can be nice and sticking up for me, like when I wanted to talk to Joel alone and Shawn didn't think it was a good idea. But then, the next minute you're saying you don't like me. If you hate me don't be nice to me, just be bitchy to me all the time, okay?"

"So you want me to be mean to you all the time like I am now."

"It would be a lot easier for me to understand you. So yeah be mean, I don't care."

"Fine if that is what you want, but remember you made the choice."

"Trust me I won't forget it. The last thing I hate about you, is when you were trying to talk Shawn into telling you what has been going on with me. Don't ever think of doing that again."

"Why can't I know?"

"Can't you get the idea of privacy?"

"Honey, when you're here you don't get much privacy."

"Well I want it. It's my business not yours, and I plan to keep it that way."

"I do have a right to know."

"No you don't. It is something in my life, not yours!" I yelled.

"Shawn will have to tell me sooner or later," She said.

"Fine you want to know? You really want to know? My stepbrother abused me. You happy now bitch!" I screamed and at that moment I got the rope loose and ran out the door. I saw that Kim had her mouth open in surprise. I went running into the woods. I kept running till I barely could breathe. So I sat down not knowing where I was and I didn't care.

Chapter 9

I just started crying and crying. I couldn't hold it in any longer, I tried I really did, but I couldn't stay strong anymore. All I could think about is how Kim is going to think of me now. I didn't want her to try and be nice to me just because of my problem, I didn't want people pitying me. I can't stand it when people do that. After about an hour or two I settled down, got a hold of myself and got up. I had no idea where I was and I turned around hoping I was going the right way. All of a sudden I stopped.

"I have a perfect chance to run away from this prison," I said to myself and then I realized I was crazy. I started walking back to the school. In about 30 minutes I reached the school and it was dark. No one was outside, so I went into the main lodge. I heard Kim and Shawn talking.

"I am so sorry Shawn. I didn't want to make her so mad, but I couldn't stand it. I am so sorry."

"Kim, one of the rules for counselors are not to criticize the students, or say bad things about them, especially to them. You know that Kim."

"I know, I know. If I knew I would make her run away I wouldn't have said anything to her."

"Don't worry I'm back," I said walking in. Shawn came over to me and hugged me.

"You didn't run away," Kim said.

"No I didn't, I just needed to get out of here. And lucky for you I did change my mind when I thought how easily I could leave, but I didn't," I told them.

"Why didn't you?" Shawn asked.

"I knew that no matter where I went I would still have every problem, plus more and besides you have helped me so much Shawn, I wanted to finish what we started," I said and Shawn smiled.

"I am glad you did come back," Kim said and went to give me a hug.

"Don't you even think about it. Just because I came back when I didn't have to doesn't mean I forgive or like you. We have a deal, you have to go through with it," I told her backing away from her.

"What deal?" Shawn asked not to happy.

"Nothing Shawn," Kim said.

"It's not nothing. He has a right to know. We made a deal, Kim told me that she wasn't too fond of me. So I told her if she didn't like me don't ever be nice to me. We made that deal that she won't act as if she likes me when she doesn't," I told Shawn and he look furious at both of us.

"I am so disappointed in both of you," Shawn said crossing his arms.

"Why?" I asked.

"First off Candy, how could you even think of such of an agreement? And Kim, my God what has gotten into you? I thought when I hired you, you were an adult. I supposedly was wrong."

"No Shawn," She said.

"No, adults especially one that is working with teenagers that could break at anytime, would ever make an agreement like that."

"Shawn I was trying to get through to her and I figured agreeing with her was the only way," Kim pleaded.

"If you two were having a problem you should have come to me."

"Shawn come on, you knew we did not like each other. Someone would have to be blind not to notice, considering I told you how I felt about her. But I do not want to talk about that now. How is Joel?" I asked.

"He is doing okay," Shawn answered.

"Where is he? Is he at the hospital?"

"No, he's in my office," He answered and I turned around.

"Where are you going?" He asked.

"Where do you think?" I said walking away.

"Candy, we are not done with this yet!" He called to me.

"We are for now," I called back and went running to Shawn's office. I walked in and Joel was lying down on the couch. I pulled a chair next to him, but he was sleeping and I didn't want to wake him. So I just sat there watching him, listening to him breathing. A little while later Shawn walked in, not looking happy.

"He fell back to sleep?" Shawn asked.

"He's been sleeping since I got in here," I whispered. "What happened to him?"

"The doctor said that he hasn't eaten in awhile, but he wouldn't tell us anything. When I asked him how he got here he just ignored me," Shawn told me.

"Kinda reminds me of someone."

"Yeah," I remarked and I knew he was talking about me. "Hey Shawn, I'm sorry I ran out of here, but I just had to get away for awhile."

"It's all right, but can you do me a favor?"

"Sure," I answered.

"Forget about that stupid deal you and Kim had, please," He pleaded.

"Fine, but I don't forgive her for anything she said to me, and I don't like her."

"I am not asking you to do any of that," He whispered. "I also don't expect you to forgive her, I wouldn't," He admitted.

"Okay," Was all I could say to him. "Are you going to make Joel leave?"

"Not yet, but I do need his phone number to call his parents, so they don't worry about him."

"It's actually only his mother and she won't even notice."

"Even so, I have to call."

"Okay it is 516-7930," I told him as he was writing it down.

"Also what is his last name?" He asked.

"It's Durent."

"Thanks kid," Shawn said as he was pushing in Joel's number. "Yes is this Ms.

Durent?" Shawn asked and I could hear Joel's mom on the other end saying,

"Yeah, what do you want?"

"Ms. Durent, my name is Shawn Jenson and I am the owner of Long Ridge. It is a school for teenagers that have problems with drugs, stealing, anorexia, and things like that."

"So get to the point!" I heard her yell.

"Well, today your son Joel showed up here."

"Why would he be there?" She yelled.

"I'm not quite sure yet, but I think it has to do with his one friend, Candy, she is a student here."

"Oh her," I heard Ms. Durent saying.

"Yeah, but he was looking really bad and he fainted, so we had doctors come, and they said that he hasn't eaten in awhile and he was also on some drugs. He is fine now; he is actually sleeping at the moment. But he is very weak."

"And what do you want me to do about it?" She said.

"Well, he is your son."

"Keep him," She yelled.

"Excuse me?" Shawn asked confused.

"I said keep him!" She screamed in the phone.

"Ms. Durent, I can't just let anyone in here. All the student's parents are paying for them to be here."

"How much is it?" She asked.

"$1500 a month," He answered. I never knew it was that much.

"Fine I'll send a check out tomorrow."

"Ms. Durent, are you sure?"

"Yeah, all that boy does around here is waste my money on drugs, so at least now he can waste my money and I don't have to take care of him. I'll also send him a check so he can get some clothes."

"All right Ms. Durent, bye," Shawn said but she already hung up. "Well, it seems that Joel is going to be staying with us," He said as he hung up the phone.

"I heard and yes. Finally I get to have a friend here," I said pleased.

"What about everyone here?"

"I mean, like a friend that I have had for awhile," I explained.

"Oh, I understand. Maybe you should wake him up," Shawn told me.

"Do you want me to tell him he will be staying here?" I asked.

"Umm…I don't think so, but you can stay here while I tell him, but when it comes to the questions the doctor asks him you have to leave."

"Can you do me a favor?"

"What?"

"Joel doesn't like doctors, so if you could can you ask him the questions like you did for me?" I asked.

"I guess," Shawn agreed. "I'll leave while you wake him up and you can talk to him while I go get the forms from the doctor that I have to ask, just don't tell him he is going to be staying here."

"Alright," I said and Shawn walked out of the door. I just sat there looking at Joel for a little bit. I couldn't believe what he did to himself. He was just lying there looking so sad, helpless, and alone. I have never seen Joel in my entire life look like he did now. He was always the strong one, the one who could make everything better and now he was the one that needs to be made better. He wasn't about to die, he wasn't even close to that, but I knew he needed help, from Shawn and maybe even from me. I tapped him on the shoulder. "Joel," I whispered. He didn't move so I said louder, "Joel," He groaned, but woke up and looked deep into my eyes.

"Candy?" He questioned. I still knew he was out of it, I have been that way many of times.

"Hey guy, how you doing?" I asked.

"I'd like to say I was fine, but I can't lie to that pretty, sweet face of yours," He answered.

"What happened to you?"

"You're going to go tell that Shawn guy," He accused me.

"Not if you don't want me to."

"Okay, well I started taking needles, and not eating very much."

"Needles?" I questioned.

"You know heroin."

"My God, Joel, I even stayed away from that stuff."

"What have they done to you, brainwashed you?"

"No Joel, I don't mean to sound all...you know, but even when I was using drugs I wouldn't do heroin. What else did you do?" I asked.

"What makes you think I did something else?"

"I know you too much, Joel."

"Fine I also did a little LSD," I was just sitting there wide-eyed. I was so shocked that I couldn't even speak. "You're going to tell that Shawn guy huh?"

"I told you I wouldn't. As much as I think I should I won't. You're my friend and I won't break your trust," I told him. I never thought I could be so disappointed in Joel. I heard a knock on the door. "Come in," I said. I was expecting to see Shawn, but it was Bryce. "Hey Bryce," I said as he came over and kissed me on the cheek.

"What's that?" Joel asked.

"Bryce is my boyfriend," I told him.

"Hey Joel," Bryce said.

"Bryce can you excuse us?" Joel asked.

"Sure," Bryce answered leaving.

"You just couldn't live without a guy. But then, I did figure you'd have a guy nailed by the end of your first week," Joel said.

"It's not like that Joel. I care about Bryce, I love him," I said getting kind of mad that he would think that badly of me.

"Yeah sure, so how many times have you done it?"

"You're still high aren't you?"

"I'm just speaking the truth."

"How could you think I couldn't love him?" I questioned getting up and walking over to the door. "And not that it is any of you're business, but we haven't done it at all," I opened the door and slammed it behind me. I couldn't believe it. I never thought I could be mad at Joel, I was wrong. Shawn walked over to me and he could tell that something was wrong.

"What's up, kid?"

"I can't believe him!" I yelled. "He actually had the nerve to say that I was lying when I told him I cared for Bryce. I just can't believe him," I said frustrated.

"Remember he is probably still high."

"I know that, but still."

"Did you happen to find out what was wrong with him?" Shawn asked.

"Yeah, but as mad as I am at him I promised him I would say anything. Besides if you check his pockets you may find what is wrong with him. Anyway before I go back in there and flip out on Joel I got to leave. By the

165

way you may want to wait till morning to tell him, he won't remember anything you say to him tonight," I told him turning and walking away. I started walking to Bryce's room, even though I wasn't supposed to be in there.

"Hey baby," I heard someone behind me say. I turned around and there was Zeke. This was the last person I wanted to see right now. He looked evil in the dark. His eyes looked almost yellow and I will say he was good looking. But there was something about him that was untrustworthy.

"Zeke, tonight is not the night to get me mad. I am in the worst possible mood, and if you get me mad I swear on everything that I have I will hit you so hard," I said.

"Oh baby Candy is sad. I feel your pain," He joked making crying sounds. I walked straight up to him.

"You sure you want to get me mad?"

"Oh I'm scared," I punched him three times in the eye saying after each punch,

"That was for Bryce, that was for me and this one is just for making me mad tonight!" And I walked away. I knocked on Bryce's door and he answered. "Can I come in?" I asked.

166

"Sure what's wrong baby?" He asked putting his arm around me.

"Hey guys," I said to everyone there. "This has been the most stressful day. First Kim, now Joel," I said leaning my head on his shoulder.

"Here sit down," He told me leading me to his bed.

"Do want us to leave?" Hobie asked.

"No, it's all right," I answered.

"Who's Joel?" Austin asked.

"He's an old friend of mine, who showed up here. And we just got in an argument," I told them. "Also Bryce you'll like this, Zeke came up to me while I was walking here."

"Why would I like that?" He asked.

"Well, he got me really mad and I punched him three times in the face," I said.

"Bravo baby," He said. All the guys except Jackson thought it was pretty good. I started to settle down after awhile and Bryce then walked me back to Shawn's office.

"What are you two still doing up?" He asked.

"Candy and I were talking," Bryce exclaimed.

"Also did you actually expect that I would be able to get to sleep," I told him. "I would be worried about him too much," I added.

"Why?" Joel asked as if he thought I hated him.

"You're my best friend, Joel; of course I am going to worry about you."

"Yeah you didn't see her earlier, when she had to be tied up because she was trying to get to you," Bryce commented as I nudged him in the side. "What?"

"Never mind."

"You were really that worried about me?" Joel questioned.

"Yeah."

"Oh, I'm sorry for what I said before. I didn't mean it," He apologized.

"It's all right," I accepted. I have learned that I never can stay mad at Joel for long; it is just so easy to forgive him. Besides the way he talks you could never say no to him.

"Hey Candy, remember who you have to talk to tomorrow," Shawn reminded me.

"My God I forgot. I do have to get to bed in that case. Why does it have to be tomorrow?" I totally forgot I had to talk to Child Services in the morning. "Well night

Shawn, goodnight Joel," I told them and waved good-bye.

"I'll walk you to your room," Bryce offered. We walked there and when we got there Bryce wished me good luck for tomorrow and gave me a goodnight kiss. I crept into the room as quietly as I could. I figured all the girls would be asleep, since it was around midnight maybe later than that. I got changed and hopped into bed. I fell asleep after awhile of worrying for Joel, and worrying about tomorrow.

Chapter 10

"Candy," I heard someone whisper and there was Kim standing over me.

"What do you want?" I asked.

"I need to talk to you," She answered.

"What time is it?"

"It's about 4:45."

"Are you kidding me, get the hell out of here. I just fell asleep about three hours ago," I told her.

"Candy, please," She begged.

"Fine if it will get you to shut up," I gave in.

"Hurry up," I got out of bed, and went into the bathroom. In about fifteen minutes I came back out. "Follow me," Kim ordered and I did what she said. We ended up at this garage thing that I have never seen open. It had all this workout equipment in it.

"What is this?" I asked and then I realized how stupid of a question that was.

"This is the place that Shawn works out at."

"Why are we here then?"

"Joel told me that before you started using drugs you use to love to work out, so I got permission from Shawn to bring you here. Let's work out," She said.

"You actually think I am going to do something with you," I said.

"Come on, you don't even have to talk to me."

"Fine," I said.

"Let's go for a run to warm up," She said starting to run.

"Alright," I said running to catch up with her. We ran to the lake and down a path into the forest. "Kim?"

"Yeah?"

"Can I do this everyday?"

"Only if Shawn or I am with you. We don't want you to run," She answered. I don't understand why I couldn't do it alone, if I was going to run I would have when I had the chance to.

"Okay," When we got done with our run we walked back to the garage place.

"Here," Kim said handing me two boxing gloves.

"What?" I asked.

"Hit the punch bag," Kim told me as if it was an order.

"You happen to have another pair?" I asked.

"Why?" She asked giving me this weird look.

"We could duke it out. I know you have always wanted to hit me, and I can't deny that I have wanted to just smack you a few times," I said.

"Even if we did have another pair of gloves, I wouldn't do that."

"Why not?"

"As much as I would love to, Shawn would kill me, plus fire me."

"Well, then you better go find some," I said.

"Very nice."

"Hey I could have said something worse. You realize I wouldn't actually duke it out with you," I informed her, but she had this look of disbelief, so I added, "When Shawn told me that he was disappointed in me, it killed me. I didn't like hearing that and I don't want to hear it again, especially from someone like Shawn."

Kim looked confused, so she asked, "What do you mean someone like Shawn?"

"An adult who believed what I said and who believed in me," I said.

"That is probably the smartest thing I've hear you say since you got here."

"Kim, let's make a deal."

"Oh no, no more deals. I was told if there were anymore deals I was gone."

"This is a good deal though."

"Let's hear it," She said.

"It's a truce. We act all friendly."

"What do you mean?"

"We act as if we don't hate each other. We act all sweet and nice, when inside we can hate each other as much as we want."

"Okay," Kim agreed as we shook hands.

"So how is it going in here?" Shawn said startling us.

"Oh hi Shawn," Kim and I said at the same time.

"What was that hand shake for? That better not have been another deal of yours," Shawn said.

"Actually it was, but before you go into a frenzy, it was a good deal. We made a truce to get along," I said as Kim nodded her head.

"Alright good, but Candy you got to leave now, so you can get cleaned up."

"Okay Shawn," I said running off to my cabin. I walked in and Kaye was sitting on her bed reading. I have notice every time I go into the room Kaye is always reading.

"Hi Candy," She greeted me.

"Hey," I answered her.

"Is C.S. coming, soon?" She asked and I knew she meant Child Services.

"Yeah, so I got to get ready," I said grabbing the clothes I set aside and ran into the bathroom to get changed and washed up. I walked out of the bathroom wearing my short-sleeve blue shirt that has flowers on it and buttons in the front. I also had my blue jeans that had flowers and plants sewed at the bottom of them.

"Good-luck Candy," Kaye said and waved good-bye.

"Thanks Kaye, I'll see you later today. I'll tell you what happens."

"Alright, bye," She said. I went running out the door and ran straight into Bryce.

"Oh I'm sorry Bryce," I apologized.

"It's all right. Are you going to Shawn's office now?" He asked.

"Yeah," I answered.

"Well, I just wanted to say good-luck, don't worry about it, and tell the truth. Yep I think that's everything," He said making me laugh.

"Thanks, but I really do have to go," I said.

"Okay, but here is a kiss for good-luck. And I will see you later."

"Bye Bryce," I said and went running off to Shawn's office. When I got there I ran in and knocked on his door.

"Come in," He answered.

"Hey, sorry it took me so long," I said to him.

"Don't worry about it, they're aren't even hear yet," Shawn said. "Now you sure you want me to stay?"

"Like I said before, if you have the time."

"All my time is yours."

"Okay, thanks."

"You're welcome," He said. "While we have the time, I need to talk to you about tomorrow."

"Yeah, my dad is coming," I said. "I already know that."

"Yeah, but you don't know why."

"He needs to tell me something. I know that too."

"But I know what he needs to tell you."

"What?"

"He'll answer that, but after he talks to you I need to tell you something very important.

He'll also hear this, but he doesn't know about it."

"Okay, sure.' Now you're going to have me wondering. At least it is just a day away," I said, as there was a knock on the door. Shawn went over to the door, but before he answered it he turned back around to me.

"You ready?" He asked.

"No, but I want to end this," I said and with that Shawn opened the door and this lady came in. I pictured it to be a man that would be coming, but I was obviously wrong. I was glad I was wrong, I would feel uncomfortable talking about this with a guy. But then, I am going to feel uncomfortable no matter what.

"Hello, Shawn," She said to Shawn and shook his hand. Then she came over to me. I stood up to shake her hand. "Hello I am Miss Baker and you must be Candace."

"Yeah," I said shaking her hand. I sat back down as she moved to the chair next to Shawn's desk. Shawn stayed standing by the door. She started setting up the video camera. I looked at Shawn and he glanced back at me. The look of his face gave me a feeling that I am going to get through this.

"This may feel weird, but we have to have a tape of this," She said and I just sat there silent. After she got it set up she sat down in the chair and pulled out a clipboard. "Could you please state your full name, and age?

"Candace Taylor Walkinson, 15 years old," I stated.

"How has your family life always been?" Miss Baker asked.

"When I was young and my parents were together I was very happy. I enjoyed being home and I loved being with my parents, but after they broke up I wasn't very happy. I still spent time with my mother, till she messed up," I said.

"What do you mean 'messed up'?" She asked.

"She was always gone, with a different guy every night, but that didn't bother me so much. When she started bring them home all the time that's when I couldn't stand being home."

"Would she sleep with those men?" She asked.

"Well, I wouldn't exactly say sleep, but they did have sex," I answered and then realized that was sort of rude. I knew she what meant in the beginning when saying sleep with them.

"Is that what bothered you?" She asked.

"Well, yeah of course it did. Having all these strange men come into my house. I felt very uncomfortable in there; it was as if it wasn't my home anymore."

"Was that the reason you started using drugs?" She asked me.

"No."

"When and why did you start using drugs?"

"My mother bringing those men home didn't bother me as much as to go and do drugs. But it did when she brought this one certain guy home. I did not like that man. When my mother told me she was going to marry him I almost flipped out. It was the worst thing possible," I said.

"Why was that bad, them getting married?" She asked me.

"It wasn't that."

"What was it?"

"It was my step brother."

"Did you not like him?"

"I hated him, I hated him with a passion," I emphasized.

"Why?"

"He would come around the house when my mother and his father would go out. While they were gone he would abuse me, and this was before the marriage. I would have told someone, but I figured it would be all over soon. See my mother never went out with a guy for very long and I figured it would be the same with this case. Well, three nights after the first time Clint abused me, my mom and his dad came home and told us that they were going to get married that night."

"Clint is your step brother right?"

"Yes, but anyway right after they said 'I do' I went to a friend's house and he had a lot of friends that did drugs. I told him to take me to one of his friend's house because I needed to hang loose and that's when and how and why I started," I finished.

"How did Clint abuse you?" Miss Baker asked.

"He would occasionally hit me, he would yell and swear at me, but most of all he would touch me," I told her.

"How so?"

"What do you mean?" I asked surprised.

179

"How did he touch you?" I felt very uncomfortable saying this and by this time I was crying.

"It's okay Candy, just take it slow," Shawn said reassuring me.

"He would touch me, I don't want to go into detail," I said feeling very, very uncomfortable.

"Well, would he make you have sexual intercourse with him?" She asked kind of helping me.

"Yeah," I said barely getting it out because I was crying so much.

"It's alright Candy," Shawn told me.

"Did he make you touch him?"

"Obviously, if he made me have sex with him, I obviously had to touch him."

"Would he give you directions on what to do?"

"What kind of questions are these?" I asked.

"Candy, she is just trying to help you," Shawn told me.

"Yes he would give me directions," I answered.

"Tell me about the first time he came in to your room and you two had sex," She said. I really didn't want to answer, but I knew I had to.

"It was during the day, my mom and his dad were on vacation and he came into my room while I was laying on my bed doing my homework. He went over to the windows and closed the shades. He came over to my bed and told me we had to talk. I was like okay. He moved my homework onto the floor. And told me that he has liked me a lot, and he asked me if I knew what people do when they like each other a lot? I was confused by the question so I just looked at him dumbfounded. He told me they make love, he asked me if I wanted to. I didn't want to hurt his feelings, but I said to him that it would be wrong because our parents are dating. He said to me that it doesn't matter, our parents aren't married, so we aren't related. I didn't want to, so I told him that I didn't think it was such a good idea. He asked me if I trusted him and I said yes. He said that if I really cared about him and trusted him it shouldn't be a problem. I still didn't want to. I shook my head no, but he wouldn't leave. He kept pestering and pestering. He said how he was sad and that I hurt his feelings. I told him I was sorry. So he put his arm around me and put his hand under my shirt. I tried to remove it, but he was too strong. He told me it was all right. He made me lay down on the bed on my back and he sat on my stomach. He took off my shirt and unbuttoned my pants. He then pulled them off. He then took off my bra and underwear. He made me undo his belt and unbutton his pants. He took them off and told me exactly what to do. Since I have never done it before he told me. I did what he said to make him leave. And we did it," I was in tears so much that I barely could see straight.

"Did you happen to record any video tapes of you two having sex?"

"Why would I? No I didn't."

"Did you ever do it outside your house?" She asked.

"Umm…yeah in his father's house, but our parent's were gone from there too."

"This may be harder than I thought without any evidence."

"Actually, Miss Baker there is evidence," Shawn popped up. Shawn looked strange, he looked as if he was crying, actually I was positive he was. Right then I knew he cared and I completely trusted him. That was hard to trust a guy again.

"What is it?" She asked and I was looking confused.

"One day I walked into my office and saw a notebook sitting on the couch. I didn't know what it was and I saw writing in it. I looked around for a name on the front page and didn't see anything. So I kind of read it and then I came across the name Clint, Joel, Brooke, and Gena. The last three are Candy's old friends and you know who Clint is. I came to the conclusion that it was Candy's diary."

"You read my diary!" I yelled out surprised.

"I'm sorry, but the day before that, she came into my office and told me about Clint and everything he did to her. I figured that if she were telling the truth it would most likely be in there. I mean I did believe her, but it is just the proof part. And I figured out that Clint was classified as S/B," Shawn said handing her the diary. I couldn't believe that Shawn would read my diary. I was just sitting there shaking my head.

"Candace, what Shawn did for you was a favor. He just made it a lot easier to prove your case and possibly win," The lady explained.

"It may have, but I am mad that he didn't completely believe me. I was misjudged about him; I believed he was the first person who believed me. Also he invaded my privacy. He now knows things about me that no one ever has. And now so will you, everyone else at Child Services, and probably the judge. Also my mother and father will have to see it. My father doesn't know very much about me and I don't want those to be the first things he finds out about me," I said.

"You're right, a lot of people will see this diary, but they will only be seeing the parts I show them. There will actually be only, Shawn, you, and me who knows every word in this diary. And I will promise you that no matter what I read in this diary I will not judge you by it or hold any of it against you," She told me.

"Neither will I. I care about every student in this school, including you. Also have I acted any different around you the past few days?" Shawn asked me.

"No," I answered back.

"If I did hold any of this against you, I would have acted different around you," Shawn told me.

"Alright," I mumbled, "I understand that you only wanted to help," I added.

"That is all I have to ask you for now," Miss Baker told me. "But you do need to sign this saying that I can take this diary."

"Okay," I said signing a sheet of paper that says I give Miss Baker permission to have this piece of evidence.

"It was good to see you again Shawn and it was nice to meet you Candace," She said smiling and shaking my hand.

"Thank you for helping," I said and she just smiled again. After she left Shawn started to apologize to me.

"Candy, I really am sorry for taking and reading your diary," There was no way I couldn't forgive Shawn.

"It's all right, I do realize you were helping," I said.

"Alright, you have to get to class. Here is your schedule and your first class is with Mitch," He told me handing me my schedule. I looked down at the schedule.

"You got to be kidding me," I said.

"What do you mean?"

"The first class I have to take is teaching me about why I should wait to have sex. I am sorry Shawn, but it's a little late."

"Just go to class," He ordered me.

"Fine, at least I'll know all the answers in the class," I proclaimed and walked out of his office. I saw Bryce waiting for me.

"Hi, how did it go?" He asked.

"Alright, I guess."

"What happened?" He questioned.

"I'll tell you about it later, but I have to get to class."

"So do I. Where are you going?" I showed Bryce my schedule. "Oh good you're going to the same place as I am."

"Really? That's great cause I have no idea where the class is."

"Oh that because it is in different places, if it is nice we're outside and if it isn't we're inside. Mitch usually tells us where we will be and today we are by the gazebo," Bryce informed me.

"Oh okay."

"Well, we better get going or we'll be late," He said grabbing my hand and we started jogging there. When we got there I saw AJ,

Hobie, Angel, Joel, and Kaye. Bryce led me over to the picnic bench where they were sitting.

"You're in our class, that is so great," Angel said with her normal perky voice.

"Yeah," I said back to her. Mitch walked over with Shawn next to him.

"Hello, class," Mitch said.

"Hi," Everyone said.

"Hey Candy, Shawn told me that I would be staying here," Joel said and I just nodded. I didn't exactly want to get into trouble the first day of my class.

"Today we will be discussing the consequences of having sex. And to do this you each will be getting a baby," Mitch said and everyone looked confused.

"I can't take care of a kid," I whispered to Bryce.

"Of course they won't be actual babies," Mitch said holding up a doll and everyone started laughing. "This dolls have a computer disk in them that will give us the information on how you took care of them. If it cries for awhile we will know. They each come with a bottle that if you hold up to their lips it will show on the disk how much you feed them. I

187

will give you your groups now. Hobie and
Angel, Kaye and Zeke," I saw the look on
Kaye's face and I felt so sorry for her. "AJ and
Bryce," When I heard that I felt so jealous. I
mean AJ and I may get along now, but I saw
how happy she looked and I still did not trust
her with Bryce.

"No, this can't be," Bryce said shaking his
head. Mitch named all the other groups.

"And the last group is Candy and Joel," I
saw the look on Bryce's face when he heard
that and he didn't look too happy. Knowing
our history I didn't really blame him.

"You two were put together. I can't believe
it. I may trust you, but I know that he likes
you," Bryce said to me.

"Yeah of course he likes me, I am his best
friend," I said to him.

"He likes you a lot more than a friend," He
whispered to me.

"No," I whispered back.

"Would you two like to grace the class with
your conversation that must be more
interesting than my discussion," Mitch said.

"No, that's alright," I said.

"Oh please tell us," He said.

"I rather not."

"If you don't share it with us you have detention."

"I'll take the detention," I said.

"Okay report here after your last class," Mitch said.

"Okay, I'll be here," I said.

"Hey sorry I got you detention," Bryce apologized.

"It's alright, I don't care," I accepted.

"Would you like to join Miss Walkinson, Bryce?" Mitch asked.

"Actually sure, why not?" Bryce answered.

"Bryce?" Shawn questioned walking over.

"Why wouldn't I want to join her?" He answered.

"Fine, come here after your last class," Mitch said.

"Okay." I was looking at Bryce in surprise.

"Now that we are quiet, please get with your partner," Mitch said. AJ and I switched spots since she was to next to Joel. Mitch passed out the kids and Joel and I got a boy.

"That's good; I always seemed to like boys better than girls," I told Joel.

"You're not kidding there," Joel said and we both laughed.

"What should we name it?" I asked.

"I don't know, you can pick. Since you are the mother, okay honey?" Joel said and I hit him. I didn't hit him hard. It was more like play fighting.

"How about Danny?" I asked.

"Oh, come on you can do better than that," Joel said.

"But you told me I could pick."

"But that is a wimpy name," Joel argued.

"Fine. How about Noah?" When he shook his head I started just naming off a lot of names. "Carter, Chase, Trent, Scout, Ian, Logan, Teck, Kyle, Clete, Cody, Ford. Well, what do you want its name to be?" I asked giving up.

"Joel Jr." He said.

"No, no, not a chance Joel."

"Why not?"

"No," I said.

"Fine name a few more and I'll say yes for one."

"Okay," I said and named a lot more and he said no to them all. "Since you can't agree with any of mine, you name some."

"Alright, Baxter," I shook my head so he named some of his. "Jordan, Theo, Miles, Colton, Damien."

"I am not naming the kid after the devil."

"Fine, Trevor, Drake, Troy, Clay, Chaz,"

"Okay Chaz will work," I concluded.

"Okay Chaz Joel Durent," Joel said.

"Joel, no we are not having your name in there."

"Fine you pick any name for his middle name, since I picked his first name and he does get my last name."

"Okay, I finally get to pick something. Chaz Noah Durent," I said.

"That is still a stupid name," When I gave Joel a mean look he added, "But I did say you could pick."

"Very good answer," I said. "So what did you name your kid," I asked Bryce and AJ.

"Candace Ashlee Ashford and you can tell who picked that name," AJ said pointing at Bryce and I just smiled. At least now I knew that even with AJ he would be thinking of me. I do trust him and I do trust AJ, but I don't trust AJ with him. I am one of the most jealous people. After Mitch passed out the kids he started talking again,

"One of you have to be with the kid at all times, even during your classes. Remember I will be grading you on what that disk says,"

191

Mitch said. "And before you leave I will be collecting them next week," As we got up to leave I heard like five kids starting to cry.

"How are we going to do this?" Joel asked.

"I don't know, I'll take the kid for today and then I'll give you it tomorrow morning to have it for the day."

"Can't you have it for tomorrow?"

"My father is coming tomorrow Joel."

"In that case yeah I'll have it tomorrow. What do you have next?" He asked.

"I actually have no idea. Let me look at my schedule," I pulled it out from my pocket. "I have math," I said happy. I love math that is one of the only subjects I am really good at. Well, actually I am better at English than math, but anyway I am good at both of them.

"Oh I have stress relief class," He said.

"What?"

"I don't know all I know is Shawn teaches it."

"Figures, he would come up with a class like that," I said.

"Candy!" I heard Bryce call. I stopped and waited for him to catch up to me.

"Where are you going?" I asked him.

"I am going to math with you," He answered.

"Oh good. You can show me how to get there. Do we have every class together?" I asked him.

"Everyone, but last class. You're last class is with Shawn, at least one a week he sees every student in Spruce Falls alone and just talks to them. It doesn't even matter about what you two talk about. And for some reason you see him twice a week," He answered.

"Oh okay. Well, see you later Joel," I said waving good-bye to him as Bryce was putting his arm around my neck and leading me in the opposite direction. "You don't like Joel, do you Bryce?" I asked him.

"I don't like some of the things he says, and for that no I really don't like him."

"What does he say that you don't like?"

"I don't like how he thinks and says how you two are going to be boyfriend and girlfriend someday. He believes that is why you two have been friends for so long," Bryce told me.

"He doesn't actually believe that will happen," I said.

"Oh yeah he does. He was just talking about it last night when I went back to Shawn's office. Shawn wasn't there, but Joel was and we started talking," As I thought about it, I did start to believe how Joel could like me.

"What else did he say?"

"You can't get mad at him for what I say."

"I won't," I promised Bryce, but I figured what I was going to hear was going to make me mad.

"I don't know how you acted around that Brent guy and to be honest I don't think I want to know. But anyway Joel said that he watched how you were around Brent and he wanted to be Brent for the longest time."

"My God!" I almost yelled and was shaking my head. "I can't believe he would actually want that. I thought Joel liked me for me," I said and Bryce looked confused. "The only way I can get you to know what I mean is to tell you about Brent."

"You can tell me, but tell me in detention today since we are at math class." The classroom was in this cabin on the boy's side of the school. "You have to go talk to the teacher."

"Who is it?" I asked.

194

"Caroline," He told me pointing to a curly, red, haired lady. I walked over to Caroline and she was facing the chalkboard.

"Excuse me Miss," I said quietly.

"Hello and it's Caroline, not Miss anything," She said.

"Oh sorry."

"Don't worry about it. Nothing big, are you new?" She asked.

"Yeah, I have been here a few days, but it is my first day of class," I told her.

"Okay, what's your name?" She asked.

"Candy Walkinson."

"I was hoping I'd get to meet you. A lot of guys in this class have been talking about you, and now I know why. You are a very pretty girl," She complemented me.

I started blushing, but I said, "Oh, thank you."

"Do you know anyone in this class?" She asked.

"Only Bryce," I answered looking around the class to make sure.

"Okay you can sit by him, but you two are not to be talking to each other. Every time someone sits by him I end up having to move one of them. He seems to talk to everyone he is near and because of that he hasn't been doing to good in this class. He is just a social butterfly," Caroline told me.

"Alright," I said laughing. I was trying to imagine Bryce as a butterfly, but I couldn't.

"You can go sit down next to him," She said pointing to the seat on the right of Bryce. I went over there and sat down.

"You get to sit by me?" Bryce asked.

"Yeah, until we start talking to each other," I said to him.

"Today we are going to learn about factoring," Caroline announced to the class and I was thinking great I already learned about this stuff and I aced the test. She first wrote a problem on the board and asked if anyone could do it. I raised my hand. "Okay Candy come on up and try it," I got up and walked to the chalkboard. The problem was to factor: $x^2-xy-30y^2=0$ the problem was so easy. I went right up there and solved it: $x^2-xy-30y^2=0$ factored equals $(x-6y)$ $(x+5y)$ and that was it. "Can you explain how you did that?"

"Oh sure. Well the problem is reverse foil, so you look at the last number and you see what multiplied by what is equal to 30 and does it add or subtract to get one, which is the middle number. Those numbers are 6 and 5; they equal 30 when multiplied and they also subtract to be 1. Then you look at the sign in front of the 30. Since the sign is a negative you now know that the 6 and 5 have to have different signs, so you now have to look at the sign in the middle and it tells you what the higher number is. The middle number is a negative, which means that the higher number, the six would have a negative sign and the lower number, five, would be the opposite or in this problem a positive. So there for, your final answer is (x-6y) (x+5y)," I explained and the teacher and class were looking at me in amazement.

"Could you do another problem and explain it step by step?" The teacher asked.

"Sure," I answered.

"Okay the problem is $5(2r-2)=r(r-1)$. Solve for x," She told me writing the problem on the board.

"Alright, the first step is to distribute the '5' in the (2r-2). And then you have to distribute the 'r' into the (r-1). Those two would make $10r-10= r^2-r$. Now you have to -10r+10 from both sides. This will make, $0=r^2-r-10r+10$. You now add the −10r and r because they are common. You get $0=r^2-11r+10$. This is also a reverse foil so you would get $0=(r-10)(r-1)$. Now you have to put both parenthesis equal to zero like this; $r-10=0$ $r-1=0$. Your answers would end up to be {10,1}." The teacher started clapping and I didn't know why.

"That was amazing," Caroline told me, "Where did you learn all of that?"

"School," I answered.

"I can't believe that you know all these things."

"I've always had a knack for math and I guess my math teacher was good," I said.

"I'll give you extra credit if you can answer this question. Okay?"

"Yeah sure."

"Okay here's the question, what are the proper or actual names for answers in factoring?" I was almost positive, but the was like 1% chance that I was wrong.

"I believe, but am not quite positive that they are called roots?" I answered like a question.

"You're right."

"Really?" I said surprised.

"Yeah."

"Cool."

"You can go sit back down now," Caroline told me. I had to say I liked this class. I went back to my seat with a smile on my face.

"I now know whom I'm going to study with for this class," Bryce whispered and I just smiled at him. At that time Bryce's baby started crying and he just looked down at it. "What am I supposed to do?" He asked me and I just shrugged.

"Bryce, what is that?" Caroline asked.

"What's it sound like to you? It's a baby, what else sounds liked that?" He said. "What am I supposed to do with it?" He asked me again.

"I don't know, how would I know anything about a baby?"

"You're a girl, isn't it just like this thing that girls have that they know how to take care of a baby?"

"Well, I didn't get it. I am horrible when it comes to kids," I told him.

"Bryce, please make it quiet," The teacher said. I guess the teacher realized it was a doll and not an actual baby.

"How? I don't know what to do," He said.

"Why do you even have a baby doll?" She asked.

199

"I love playing with dolls," He joked, but he actually never said the exact reason.

"In one of our classes we were given a baby to take care of for a week. We are graded on it," I explained and at that time my baby started crying.

"Oh great, now we have two," One of the girls in front said.

"Oh be quiet," I told her lifting my baby up. I held it and rocked it back and forth and it quieted down.

"What did you do? How did you do that?" Bryce asked.

"I just rocked it back and forth," I answered. Bryce grabbed the baby by the arm and swung it back and forth. "No, Bryce like this," I said grabbing the doll out of his hand. I rocked the thing back and forth like I did with mine and the thing became silent again. Bryce was looking at me in admiration.

"Thank you, Candy," The teacher said as I was handing the sleeping doll back to Bryce. I kept mine sitting on my lap, just in case it did start crying again it was already there.

"Thanks," Bryce said.

"Welcome," After math class was over Bryce and I had gym with Shawn teaching. "Where is the gym class held?" I asked him.

"Over by the lake," He answered.

"Okay well at least I know where that is," I said.

"Well, it took you long enough to figure out where things were," Bryce joked.

"Very funny," I said hitting him in the shoulder; not hard though.

We walked hand in hand over to the lake. Shawn was there obviously, since he was the teacher. Also AJ and Austin were in our class. I couldn't really imagine AJ participating in gym class, but then I never did at my old school. I could have participated; I was always good in sports. I just never wanted to actually do anything in the class, besides I did not want to get changed, unless it was in the guy's locker room. And you can guess that the teachers didn't go to well with that idea.

"Hey everyone, could you all just sit down for a second," Shawn said and everyone sat down on the ground. "Thanks, we have a new student that some of you probably already know. Her name is Candy, would you please stand up Candy?" I wanted to say no, but I didn't think it would be too good to get two detentions in one day. I stood up and said hi and then sat back down.

"I hate all the teachers announcing that I am a new student, like people are that dumb not to tell," I whispered to Bryce who just smiled at me.

"Today we will be starting a new unit, we will be playing football," Most of the guys cheered and almost all of the girls groaned. "And for all you guys cheering, it will not be tackle. We are playing flag football. It's no different than regular football except that to stop a person from running you don't tackle them you grab their flag. Okay?" Everyone nodded. "Who wants to be captains?" Bryce and Austin were the only ones who raised their hands. "Okay heads or tails, Austin you call."

"Tails," Austin said.

"It's heads, Bryce you pick first and whether you want to be the kicking or receiving team."

"We will receive."

"Okay start picking."

"I choose Candy," Bryce said for his first pick. I was happy. They chose all the other people and I was glad that AJ wasn't on our team.   "Okay so who wants to be the quarterback?" He asked and no one raised his or her hand.

"I will," I said.

"Okay," Bryce answered.

"Wait you're going to have a girl play quarterback?" One of the guys asked.

"Did you happen to see that game I was playing a few days ago?" Bryce asked. The kid said yes, "Well the person who scored most of the touchdowns was her. So, I'd advice you to shut your mouth and play," Bryce said and I just smiled at him. When we starting playing the other team made the kick off and Bryce caught it and ran quite far, so when I moved in it made it a lot easier. I got the ball and no one seemed to be open to throw it to, so I just ran it all the way and made a touchdown. Everyone on my team started cheering for me and I loved it. After gym we had lunch. The whole school has lunch at the same time, which I thought was cool. After lunch the day went by pretty quick. I had Biology after lunch, then I had Global History, then study hall, then I had to go to Shawn's office for my last class. It was the class that Bryce was telling me about. I knocked on the door and Shawn said to come in.

"Hi Shawn," I said cheerfully.

"Hi, I see you had a good day, and good-job in gym, you surprised a lot of the guys."

"Oh thanks," I figured that this was the easiest class.

"I heard Bryce telling you about this class and I know you are thinking two questions because every student has these one you are graded and two there is homework." He was right those were the two questions that I had.

"Homework?"

"Yes there is homework. I give each student a totally different project and I will tell you yours now because I knew it the day you walked into this school what it was going to be. Your project is actually harder than most and that is one of the reasons why you are here two times a week unlike everyone else who are here once."

"Okay, so what is it?" I asked.

"I want you to somehow right a letter, diary entries or something like that on this year. Like you coming here and how you have changed," Shawn said.

"Oh okay, that shouldn't be too difficult," I said.

"Really you don't think so?"

"All it is, is writing and that is my best subject, that and math I am good in."

"I have a question I ask this to everyone. What do you want to be?"

"I want to be a young adult fiction novelist."

"Whoa and you have the whole name of it. Most people would say a writer and leave it at that."

"Well, I know exactly what I want to be and that is it. You asked a questions and I answered it honestly."

"And I respect that."

"You don't know how much that means to me," I told him.

"If you couldn't be a writer what would you want to be?" Shawn asked.

"Well, let me think. I'd like to be an actress that would be cool. I want to have a job in entertainment of some sort. An actress, writer, maybe a singer."

"You're good at singing?" He asked.

"I was told by Joel that I was and I don't think he would lie to me about that," I answered.

"I never knew that. Could you sing something?"

"Now?" I questioned.

"Yeah."

"No, wait no. I can't sing in front of people. Joel I did sing in front of because we were in the car and I didn't even notice that I was singing to the radio. But I get way too nervous."

"But you're like a social butterfly. You can strike up a conversation with almost anyone."

"I can talk and talk, that I know. But talking has no talent involved in it, singing does. If I could I would sing for you, but I can't."

"It's alright. Well class is over. I'll walk you to your detention with Mitch and also you don't have to do kitchen duty anymore. I am giving you a break, because it was only your second day or something like that when you broke the rules," Shawn told me.

"Oh thank you so so so so so much."

"You're so so so so welcome," We walked to where Mitch was and we were kind of late.

"I was just going to go to Shawn and tell him you skipped your detention."

"No, she's okay. It's my fault she is late," Shawn said.

"Okay go sit down by Bryce and *no* talking to him," Mitch said pointing to Bryce. Bryce was lying down on the grass; he was messing with a piece of grass. I walked over to him and smiled at him. He put his arm around me and hugged me. I put my head on his shoulder and just kept it like that for awhile. I heard Mitch questioning about Bryce and me. Shawn told him that we are going out and it is okay how we were that close. I was happy how Shawn always seemed to stand up for me. It made me feel really good.

"You two can talk, but only till I am done talking with Shawn," Mitch told us.

"You were going to explain why you couldn't believe why Joel wanted what Brent had," Bryce said.

"It's just that Brent and I did many things I regretted. I didn't care about Brent and he didn't care about me. And I kind of explained to you what we did together, right?" I asked he nodded his head, "I care about Joel, he is my best friend. He is like you except I have more

207

emotion in how I care about you. Both of you I can tell anything to. But I just couldn't believe that he would want to do what I did with Brent rather than having me care about him."

"Oh okay, I understand now. So that is why he doesn't like me too much."

"Joel likes you," I told him surprised to hear what he said.

"He doesn't hate me, but he doesn't exactly want to be my friend."

"Joel isn't really the kind of person who has friends, he is the kind of person who hangs out with everyone. I was really his only permanent friend," I explained.

"Till you see him today, you mean."

"Oh I didn't mean that. No I will always be his friend. That will never change," I said.

"Okay good. I didn't want to just ruin a lifetime friendship," Bryce said to me.

"Okay, you two have to be silent now," Mitch said.

"I kept him busy as long as I could," Shawn told us smiling.

"Candy, I want you to fill out this," Mitch told me handing me a packet.

"What is it?" I asked.

"It is just a little test to see how much you know about sexual transmitted diseases and about safe sex. Just things like that. You won't be graded on it; it is for me to see how much you know. Everyone had to take them," He explained. I opened the packet and the first question was what percent of minors have sex with people over 18 year olds. I had no idea the answer, which wasn't the greatest thing. I always feel horrible when I can't figure out the first question. I chose the answer c, because I heard that the general percentage of wrong answers were actually c when right, so I picked that. When I finished Bryce and I were free to go.

"So how do you think you did?" Bryce asked. I just gave him this look and he knew the answer. "I didn't do too good when I took it either."

"What did you get?" I asked.

"A 20%."

"Not good," I said and he shook his head to agree.

"Let's go to the lake," Her grabbed my hand and we went running off. When we got there we sat down. He had his arm around me and I had my head on his shoulder.

"Bryce?"

"Yeah," He answered.

"I have been wondering this ever since I got here."

"What?" He asked.

"How did you end up here?" I asked.

"Like I told you the day you came here. My father called and Travis and Paul came and got me," He said.

"Well, I mean what did you do that your had dad to call here?" I realized it wasn't exactly any of my business to ask him, but he knew everything about me getting here. He didn't answer me for awhile, I figured he didn't want me to know. "I was just asking, because I couldn't imagine you doing anything bad."

"I was into some heavy drugs and I did some bad things to people while I was using."

"Oh."

"I want to tell you something, but I am afraid of what you'll think of me," Bryce said.

"Bryce, you know all the things I did, it can't be very much worse than that."

"Well, you know how you use to sleep around? Well, I was the same way, except I had a girl friend. I hurt her really bad by doing that. A friend if hers told her that she saw me with the perky blonde girl. I was apparently leading her up the stairs to a friend's room. I just barely could remember the girl I led up those stairs, but then when I saw you it reminded me of that girl," Bryce said and it was weird. I didn't want to remind him of the girl that made him and his girlfriend break up, but after that it got even worse.

"Why did I remind you of that girl?" I asked.

"That girl was…you. That is what I had to talk to Shawn about the day you came."

"What!" I yelled.

"I should have told you."

"But you didn't. Is it just now you are going out with me, because of what I did before," I said jumping up and went running to my room. I ran in and AJ and Kaye were there. They both realized that I was looking mad.

"What's up?" They both asked at the same time.

"I just can't believe it. I can't believe he didn't tell me. How could he do that? I thought he was different," I kept saying these things over and over.

"Who?" AJ asked.

"Bryce who else," I answered. AJ went walking out of the room.

"Okay, now that she's gone what's up?" Kaye asked.

"You know how I slept around right?"

"Yeah."

"Well, he was one of the guys and I never knew it. He knew it since the first day I was here, he told Shawn, yet how could he not tell me. How could Shawn not tell me? Bryce apparently led me up some stairs and because of me he hurt his girl friend. How could I have, how could he have?" I asked out loud.

"Well, you both were on a lot of drugs I am guessing."

"Me more so than him, since I couldn't remember and he could. The thing that I am wondering is does Bryce really care about me or can he remember enough to know what we did," I said and then I started crying. Kaye moved over to me and put her hand on my shoulder.

"Oh, he really does care about you."

"How do you know?" I asked.

"The way he looks at you, the way he always seems to manage to touch your hand.

He loves you girl. Also when he was with Angel he didn't do any of that. I never saw them holding hands or anything."

"That's odd," I commented.

"Why?"

"Football Jock and Cheerleader, it seems kind of obvious that they'd be together. You know as an image," I said.

"You know better than that. Bryce is not like that," She said and there was a knock at the door. I was still crying so I tried to wipe the tears off my face.

"Is Candy here?" I heard Bryce say.

"Yeah," Kaye said with an attitude. I could tell that she was about as mad as I was.

"Can I please talk to her?" He asked.

"Candy, you want to talk to Bryce?" She asked me.

"I guess," I said still crying.

"Alright, I'll leave you two alone. And if you hurt her I'll kill you myself," She whispered to him, but I still could hear her.

"Candy?" He said as a question.

"What?" I answered quietly.

"I'm sorry; I know I should have told you about it. I just didn't want you to feel bad about me. I know how much you hate Brent, because he only liked you for one reason and I didn't want you to think that was why I like you."

"It isn't?" I asked.

"No, I can't even remember what it was like that night. I actually care about you. I love you, Candy. I have never said that to anyone," He explained.

"I love you too," I said back. "I am also sorry, it was as much of my mistake as it was yours."

"Okay, so stop crying and let's go for a walk," Bryce requested holding out his hand.

"All right," I said putting my hand in his. As we were walking a couple of his friends stop to talk to him. One of them almost dragged him away saying that Harrison needed to talk to him about something very important. Bryce said good bye to me and went running off to his room. I wondered what could be so important. It wasn't any of my business, so I didn't follow them. I kept walking and I ended up bumping into Shawn and actually I did literally bump into him.

"Hey kid, you better watch where you are going," He said with a smile on his face.

"Shawn, why didn't you tell me about Bryce knowing me before we came here?" I asked.

"It wasn't my place to tell you. It was his."

"Oh, I was just wondering," I said.

"You're not mad at me are you?" He asked.

"No not at all. I was just surprised you didn't mention anything to me. I mean I wish you did, but I don't blame you for it," I told him.

"Well, I am glad you're not mad."

"You should realize I can't stay mad at certain people. There are three people that have that power over me, Bryce, Joel, and you."

"Oh, at times that may not be good, but the three people that have this power over you are three very trusting people."

"Well, I am going to go to my room, so I'll talk to you later, bye Shawn," Shawn waved and said good bye to me too. I walked into my room and May was there. I rarely ever talked to May.

"Hi Candy," She greeted me.

"Hi."

"Candy, I noticed me and you never really talk to each other. I understand why, you told us why when you first came here. I want you to know this first if you ever do need to talk to anyone I am here. I may not really ever act like I care, but it is just that I don't go bugging people about there problems, like Angel does," May said and I was surprised that she talked bad about a person.

"Thanks." I said.

"I need to ask a favor from you."

"What?" I asked.

"Well, Shawn's birthday is coming up next week and I wanted to set up a huge party for him. Well, I was talking to your friend Joel and he told me that you were a great singer. I was hoping you could sing lead to this song I picked out and have the rest of our group sing the chorus as a gift to Shawn," She asked. "Please?"

"May, I can't sing in front of people, I have never sang in front of people."

"But we have a week to work on that, please please please," She begged.

I gave in, "I'll try, but I'm not guaranteeing anything."

"Oh my God, thank you so much. Well, let's go start working. We have permission from Kim to work in the cafeteria; all the

Spruce Falls are there. That is why Bryce had to quickly go off." That is why he went running off I thought. "You have to learn the whole song. I hope you don't mind that all these people will be there."

"How many people are you talking about?" I asked.

"Me, Kim, Joel, Bryce, and the rest of Spruce Falls," She told me.

"Okay," I said kind of scared of all these people being there. We walked over to the cafeteria and it looked so different, since there was no one there.

"Hey everyone, Candy agreed to sing the part," May announced to everyone. Everyone just cheered. Bryce walked over to me and gave me a hug.

I hugged him back and said, "Hi."

"Hey baby, here is the music you'll be singing," He said handing me a paper. I knew the song; it was *Wing Beneath My Wing*. I heard it sung by Bette Midler before. I really liked it.

"Do you know the song?" May asked.

"Umm...most of it, I can't exactly sing it by heart, but I know it enough," I answered.

"That's good," May said. "Well, I am guessing we should start getting you to learn it and your parts."

"Sounds good to me."

"Okay, you just look at the paper while we sing our parts. We'll skip through it or even better; Kim can you sing her parts?" May asked.

"Sure," Kim answered. They had the one girl from my math class that made the remark about our dolls making noise playing the piano. The chorus that everyone sang was very good, but I didn't like Kim's voice. She tried too hard and it came out yucky. After they finished I had notes all over my paper. It said where I was to sing and not sing or where I lower my voice so the chorus can join me.

"Is that all clear?" Kim asked expecting me to say no.

I held up my paper with all the notes and said, "Got it all, crystal clear."

"So you ready to sing?" May asked.

"Yeah, I think I am." They started playing the song and when I started to sing I was so surprised that wasn't really really nervous. I didn't even mess up once. I was even more surprised when the chorus part came and no one started they were all listening to me sing. I just kept going as if they were suppose to stop there. When I was done everyone started clapping, even Kim.

"Wow, that was amazing," Angel said.

"Even better than the first time I heard you sing," Joel commented.

"Thanks everyone, I haven't sang in awhile I was surprised I still could."

"Candy, can you do that one more time and since everyone has heard what she sounds like, let's all of sing this time," May said. We sang all through it.

"How did you like it?" May asked me as if I was the director of this thing.

"It sounded great to me."

"Same with me," Kim put her two cents in. "Candy, I love your voice. It is really good. If you were to work with me in singing maybe we can take that voice somewhere," She offered.

"No thanks, Kim. I don't want a career on my voice," I answered kind of mad that she thought she could do anything with my voice. I didn't even like hers and I didn't want to start sounding like her.

"Alright I was just trying to be helpful."

A. M. Lahrs

"Okay," I answered simply.

Chapter 11

That night when I fell asleep all I could think about was singing and of course my dad coming. I couldn't wait. I missed him so much, also I wanted to know what Shawn meant by him having to tell me something important. I didn't know whether to be worried or feel happy, but it didn't stop me from falling asleep.

"Wake up, you're dad's here," Kim said shaking me.

"Okay," I said jumping out of bed, "Give me about 15 minutes."

"Okay, but try and hurry up," She said leaving. I went looking through all my clothes and I found the perfect thing to wear. It was my blue and green Hawaiian sundress. It was spaghetti-strap and was a little above me knees, but not too much. I did my make-up and put my hair up and had all these cute butterfly clips. I also put the butterfly necklace on that he gave me for my last birthday. I looked in the mirror and said out loud to myself, "I look perfect." I put my nice dress shoes on and went running out the door. I almost tripped down the stairs, so I thought it best to walk not run. I walked into Shawn's office and my dad was sitting down in the chair. He look nothing different from the last time I saw him, dark brown hair, blue eyes, and as handsome as he has ever been.

"Dad," I said as he got up to give me a hug. He picked me up and twirled me around and when he put me down he said,

"Oh my, you look so beautiful and grown up, I can't believe my little girl is all grown up, and looking perfect as ever. You must make all the guys here go crazy." I could tell I was blushing.

"Actually she has had an impression on all the guys here, especially the one she is dating." Shawn answered.

"You have a boyfriend here?" He asked smiling.

"Yeah," I said and I noticed how sweet and innocent I sounded. That was the first time in awhile I felt sweet and innocent.

"What's his name?"

"Bryce Ashford," I answered.

"I think I may just have to meet him." I was so happy to have someone say that. I know how all girls when they have a boyfriend their parents want to meet them. I have never had that and it made me feel left out, so it was great having someone concerned about me.

"How about you show your father around before we talk?" Shawn suggested.

"Okay, come on Dad," I said and my dad took my hand and I felt as if I was a little girl again walking somewhere with my dad where he had to hold my hand. If only it was true.

"So, how do you like it here?" My dad asked as we were walking out of the office.

"It is really nice here. At first I hated it and wanted to go back home, but then I opened up to the people here and noticed that they were going to help me. It's my new home and my new family here. Besides I have a lot of fun here and I am one of the smartest people here; which I love," I answered him.

"You always did love attention."

"Who doesn't?" I asked.

"Good point, so let's see this place."

"Okay," I took him to the main lodge, my room, the lake, the forest, I showed him all over.

"This really is a nice place, I see why you like it here," He commented.

"There's Bryce, you said you wanted to meet him." I said and called him over, "Bryce this is my father, dad this is Bryce."

"Hello Mr. Walkinson," Bryce said shaking his hand.

"Nice to meet you Bryce."

"I'm sorry I actually have to go I have a class and if I am late I'll be getting detention and I don't want that. It was nice to meet you Mr. Walkinson. I'll see you later, Candy, and you look really cute in the dress," He told me.

"It was good to meet you too," My father said and Bryce went running to class. "He seems very nice."

"He is, he's perfect."

"What are some of the classes like here."

"Well, they have the same one's as in school, like math, English, stuff like that. But then, they have other classes, like dangers in sex, stress management, and Shawn meet's with everyone once a week, but for some reason he meets with me twice. I never actually found out the exact reason why," I told my dad.

"You just seem to have a full schedule here," My dad commented.

"I think they do that so we have no time to think of anything bad like drugs and stuff."

"It makes sense."

"Yeah, well, that's all there really is to see here, so maybe we should go back to Shawn's office to talk."

"Yeah that is a good idea, cause I actually have to get going."

"You can't stay long?" I asked.

"No, you know how my job makes me travel all the time. Well, that is the only reason I could come here, cause I was passing through here," He told me and it made me sad. We walked into Shawn's office and he was sitting at his desk on the phone.

"Hang on one second and I'll be with you two," He told us. We both took a seat on the couch and waited for him. He hung up the phone and apologized, "Sorry about that, but I had to take that call."

"It's alright," Both my dad and I said.

"Okay, so Mr. Walkinson you have told me what you needed to tell Candy, but like you requested I didn't tell her. And after you are done talking to her I need to talk to you both about it," Shawn said and my dad nodded.

"Okay, I'm in the dark," I said.

225

"Sweetie, I have something very important and sad to tell you," My dad informed me.

"What?"

"You're mom called me up the day you told her about Clint and his problem and she told me she couldn't take care of you. She said either I have to get full custody of you or she was going to put you up for adoption." I gasped at the thought of adoption. Me be adopted wasn't going to happen. "The real bad part is that as much as I want you to be with me, I can't take you. I travel way too much; I also don't have enough money to support you. I'd end up ruining your life. There is no other choice for me then to tell your mother that I can't take you. I will have to call her tomorrow to tell her. Honey, please stop crying," He pleaded, but I couldn't. I was an unwanted child.

"But I have another choice instead of adoption. This was what I wanted to talk to you both about," Shawn spoke up.

"What?" My dad questioned.

"I care for Candy as if she was my own daughter. I don't want her to be adopted, so I have thought about this greatly. I want to become her full guardian. I already got the papers for it and I even did research to make sure I'd be able to. All we need is a court date with you and her mother and it can be settled. Candy if you want to I would love to be your guardian?" Shawn asked me.

"Really? You want me?" I questioned.

"You're making yourself sound as if you're an item to be bought, but yes I would love to have you come and be with me. Obviously, I would be keeping you in this school till you graduate, but for holidays and after you graduate I would love for you to live with me," Shawn said, "So what do you say?"

"I say thank you," I got up and gave Shawn a hug.

"So that is a yes?" Shawn asked.

"Yeah," I answered.

"Well, I am glad, now I can still see you if I am ever in town," My dad said, "And Candy, I hope you're not mad at me cause I can't take you."

"No, I understand why you can't."

"I am so sorry, but I have to go. I have a huge meeting tomorrow and I have to get to the other side of the state for it. So Candy, I will miss you and I'll keep in touch," He said and gave me a goodbye hug. "And Shawn it was nice meeting you and I'll call you to see when we can get this court date. I'll make some phone calls and call Candy's mother. And thanks a lot," He said shaking Shawn's hand. "Bye sweetie," He waved to me.

"Bye dad," I whispered to myself. "So you are going to be my guardian," I turned to Shawn.

"Yep, seems so," He answered and smiled.

"So guardian, can I get the rest of the day off since I only have about 2 mods left?" I asked expecting a no.

"I guess."

"What? Really?"

"Yeah, really. Now get out of here before I change my mind," He said and I went running out of his office to my cabin. Angel was in there laying down crying.

"Angel, what's wrong?" I asked moving over to her bed. She rolled over and I saw this huge bruise on her face. "Who did that to you?" I asked.

"I was skipping class with Zeke and he took me into one of the sheds and he wanted to do it and I told him no. I didn't want to." I didn't need to hear the rest I jumped up and went running out of the door. I have had enough with Zeke. He was going to pay this time. I saw him over at the basketball court with a couple of his friends.

"You bastard!" I screamed, "What the hell is wrong with you?"

"What are you talking about?" He asked.

"As if you don't know! What you did to Angel was wrong."

"Oh that, well, she deserved it. That girl should learn her role in life."

"What did you say?" I have always hated when someone said that a girl has one role in life. Someone told me that and let's just say I don't know where I got all that rage from, but he couldn't walk without looking like a penguin for a week.

"I said that she should learn her role in life and so should you."

"Oh no, you did not just say that!" I yelled and jumped at him. Someone came running over to me.

"Candy, he isn't worth it," I noticed the voice as Kaye's.

"Let me go! He may not be worth it, but he sure as hell deserves it!"

229

"Candy come on." She had me around the waist and I just couldn't get loose. "Come on, before you get in trouble."

"Okay," I answered so she let me go and I went running back at him and jumped at him, but he grabbed hold of me and threw me to the ground and left with his friends. But before he left he said one thing that just made me really mad, especially since I had no idea how he knew about it,

"No wonder why Bryce slept with you in the first place a few years ago. You're rough and that is probably what he was looking for."

"You ass," I said trying to get up to go after him, but Kaye stopped me.

"No, don't. He is just trying to get to you."

"It's working," I said pushing the hair out of my face. My dress was ripped on the side and I had a huge scrape along the side of my leg.

"Come on let's get you cleaned up. You may have to put some cover-up on to hide the scratch you got on your forehead," She informed me. I reached up and touched where the scratch was and when I pulled my hand away it stung and I saw blood on my hand.

"Oh man, Shawn is gonna kill me," I remarked.

"Only if he finds out."

"I don't think I can lie to him," I told her.

"I'm not saying lie to him, just don't tell him. . If he asks tell him, but if he doesn't why bother," She told me and gave me a sneaky glare. "Now let's go get you some makeup so he won't ask anything and don't go .wearing shorts." We walked to our room and Angel was still there, but she wasn't crying anymore. We walked into the bathroom and Kaye whispered, "What happened to her?"

"You don't know?" And she shook her head. "Well, I don't know if I should tell you without her permission, but I'll give you a hint."

"Okay what is it?" Kaye asked.

"Did you think there was no particular reason I went after Zeke?"

"He hit her?"

"Yep."

"Oh, Shawn's gonna kill him."

"No he won't. She's not going to tell him," I said.

"She's got to, Cause if she doesn't he's going to do it again to her."

"Trust me I know this. I'll talk to her during dinner. I'll be able to get some sense in her. Tell Shawn something, so he doesn't come looking for us or whatever."

"Okay, but how are you going to get her to tell him?" Kaye asked.

"Remember I've already been through this. Besides I can persuade girls to do things, just as much as I can guys," I told her.

"Here you barely can even tell you got hit," Kaye said and I looked in the mirror and she was right.

"Whoa, not bad, not bad at all. Thanks Kaye. Now you better get to dinner before Shawn comes looking for you," I told her and she went running off. I walked out of the bathroom and Angel was still lying on her bed. "Hey Angel." She didn't answer, "I know you're faking it so don't even try to pretend you're sleeping. I have done it many times, so don't even try it on me. Now get up and look at me." She opened her eyes and sat up, "Good, now see how easy that was. The bruise is pretty bad let's get some makeup on it. Come to the bathroom with me." She got up and followed me into the bathroom.

"If you are going to try and talk me into telling Shawn forget it. I'll get in trouble for skipping class and also for sneaking into the shed with Zeke," She told me and tears weld up in her eyes.

"Yeah, but you want this happening again, cause trust me if you don't say anything now he'll do it again to you. Zeke is strong, trust me, I know." I pulled my pants down, so she could see what he did to me.

"You went after him?" She asked.

"When I saw what he did to you is was like seeing the same thing again and I couldn't handle .that, so yes I did go after him," I answered her.

"What do you mean the same thing again?" She asked.

"Come, take a walk with me," I ordered her and she followed my instructions. We walked into the forest. "I am going to tell you this, but you have to swear not to tell anyone, okay?"

"Yeah sure," She promised.

"My step brother Clint has abused me since before his father and my mother got married which was awhile ago. He is technically part of the reason I started using. He hurt me more than you can even imagine, physically,

233

mentally, and emotionally. He has punched me, kicked me, slapped me, pushed me into walls, and he has even hit me with things," I told her.

"You should tell someone," She said to me.

"Why?" I asked.

"Because if you tell someone he won't be able to hurt you anymore. And if you're not around he'll hurt someone else. Plus it will get it off you're chest...wait I see what you're doing, you're trying to make me take my own advice. It's not going to work. And it wasn't nice to lie about something like that."

"Angel, does it look like I am lying to you. Well, I'm not, that has actually happened to me, but I have already told Shawn about it and he has helped me," I told her.

"Well, I am not telling him this."

"Then let me put it this way to you, Angel!" I yelled, "Do you want to be hurt, you thought that bruise was bad, well, think again sweetie. He'll hurt you worse the next time and I am speaking from my own experiences. Do you want it to be to the point where when someone walks behind you and you cower down? Or if a guy that really likes you tries to hug you push him away and lose him forever? I do not want to see you go through what I have, so if you don't go tell Shawn right now, the rest of your life will be a living hell and trust me when I say I am not exaggerating about this." I lectured to her and I wouldn't be surprised if the whole school heard me.

"Okay, I'll go tell him if you come with me," She gave in.

"If that's what you want," I answered back. We walked to Shawn's office in silence. "Hey DeDe what's up?" I said to Shawn's secretary. She was a very old lady and very nice too. I was in here so much we got beyond first name basis and talked very much.

"Hey sweetie, I'm doing good," She answered.

"Is Shawn in his office?" I asked.

"No he's in the cafeteria right now. I think you are suppose to be too," She said giving me an, 'it's okay I won't tell' smile.

"Well, can you do that little page thing to get him here it is kind of an emergency?" I asked her.

"For you I'd call anyone you want here."

"Thanks Dede. You still working on getting my favorite band for me?"

"Yeah, they really are hard to do the page thing to," She joked. She knew who my favorite band was, so we always joked about how she was going to get them for me. "He should be here any moment, Candy. Go in and make yourself at home," She said to me, "Oh and here's that candy that you love so much," She said tossing me a bag of Jelly Bellys, "But if Shawn asks you…"

"I didn't get them from you," I finished her sentence.

"Very good." I put the bag of candies in my pocket and took Angel into Shawn's office.

"You are on first name basis with Shawn's secretary?" Angel asked.

"Actually we are past first name basis, DeDe isn't her first name, but her first and last name begin with a D so I call her DeDe. We're close here; I am in here so much that we started talking," I told Angel as Shawn walked in.

"Hi girls, what's up?" Shawn asked.

"Angel wants to tell you something and I am here for moral support," I answered.

"Oh okay, so what's up Angel?" Shawn asked. Angel told him the whole story about skipping class, sneaking into the shed, and what Zeke tried to make her do, and then what he did to her when she said no. I just sat there quietly and listened. When she was done I spoke up,

"Doesn't it sound familiar, Shawn?" And when he gave me a weird look about saying it in front of Angel I added, "She's knows about it."

"Yeah she told me her story when she was persuading me to tell you. Because of her I came to tell you," Angel informed Shawn.

"Good job Candy, maybe I should have you teaching a class here since you are doing so good."

"Could I?" I asked.

"I'll think about it, but back to Zeke," Shawn said.

"Yeah what are you going to do with him?" I asked.

"I have no other choice then to send him a juvenile detention home," Shawn said.

"Ha, he has to go to Juvy. That may seem mean, but he sure does deserve it," I commented.

"Yes he does deserve it. I did give that kid way too many chances. Candy I know what you can teach, but it will be after all your classes," Shawn told me.

"Okay cool, what is it?" I asked.

"Well, since you seem to have a way with persuading people, so every kid that has detention will come to you during it. I will give you your own office and everything," Shawn said and I was ecstatic, "I figure sending the bad kids to you will be there first set of punishment and if you are doing really good with them I will make it their last punishment. And if you can't do anything then they go to Juvy."

"Oh this is too cool. When do I start?"

"I guess tomorrow after school," He answered.

"Can we go get my office ready now?" I asked.

"Wait, I still need to talk to Angel about this. Go ask my Ms. Drake to show you the empty office while I talk to Angel, okay?"

"Okay, sure," I said and walked out of his office. "Hey DeDe Shawn was wondering if you could show me the empty office. I am going to be working in there from now on. I think you should be my new secretary," I said to her.

"I'll talk to Shawn about it. Come on it's this way," She said leading the way. It was on the other side of the building as Shawn's office was. I walked in and it was as big as Shawn's office, but it looked a lot nicer. Like Shawn's it had a couch, two chairs, and then one big, comfy, gray chair behind a nice, big desk. I sat down in the comfy chair and twirled around.

"I could get use to this," I said to DeDe and she smiled at me.

"You remind me so much of my granddaughter when she was your age. The long blonde hair, bright blue eyes. The guys all loved her too. Oh I miss her so much."

"How old would she be?" I asked.

"Oh at least 21 years old. She's a model, don't ya know."

"Really? I always wanted to be a model, but never even got a chance. Especially after I started to use drugs. I wouldn't have been able to recognize a catwalk from a highway let alone trying to walk down either of them," I joked.

"You have a sense of humor like she did too."

"Why haven't you seen her at all?"

A. M. Lahrs

"When she was about sixteen her mother and I got in a huge fight and she moved away and I never have gotten to see her since then," DeDe told me and she looked so sad.

"What's her name?"

"Emma Drake."

"That name has a perfect ring to it," I said and DeDe nodded.

"Well, I better be getting back to work, bye sweetie."

"Bye DeDe, it was nice talking to you," I said.

"And it was perfect as always talking with you honey. I'll see you later," She said waving goodbye and I waved back to her. She really was a sweet old lady. Shawn just then walked in breaking my thoughts.

"Hey Shawn, this office is perfect. Thank you."

"Not a problem, and you can keep this job for as long as you like, but if your grades start slipping then you'll have to give it up," Shawn said.

"Okay," I agreed. "I was saying to DeDe that she should be my secretary."

"You two really do get along. You're going to probably hate it when she leaves."

"What do you mean when she leaves?" I asked completely lost.

"She is retiring after this year is over," Shawn answered.

"I can't believe it. We have to have a goodbye party for her. Can we?" I begged.

"Wait till the time starts to come and ask me again."

"Okay."

"I want to thank you for persuading Angel to come and tell me what happened. How did you do it?" He asked.

"I told her about my problems leaving out the part that I told you. So she told me I should tell someone and I asked why. Then she realized what I was doing and she said it wasn't going to work. She thought I was lying about the story, so I told her it was true. After she said she wasn't going to tell you, I got annoyed and started yelling at her about how she thought the bruise on her face was bad well that was nothing and stuff like that. I told her if she didn't tell you her life would be a living hell, not even exaggerating and she then decided to tell you. So basically I was nice, I used my problems and her advice to them, and

A. M. Lahrs

when all that failed, I yelled," I told him and he laughed.

"Well, it did work, so when I have the people come to you tomorrow do whatever you did to Angel."

"I'll try my best and hopefully that will be good enough."

"I'm sure you'll do fine. If I know you as well as I think I do you won't let yourself do bad," Shawn said and he was right. I was never the type of person who would let myself do badly without a fight. I can't stand disappointing people cause I wasn't good enough.

"I hope I do good and can help people. Shawn I have a question and I mean I may change my mind in a couple of years, but I figured I should start thinking of my future early, so I have some idea of what I am going to do with my life."

"Okay, well what's the question?" He asked.

"Well, I am guessing you will be my complete guardian till I turn 18 and am not considered a minor, but even when I am 18 you'll probably still treat me as if you are my guardian, right?"

242

"Yeah, probably. Was that it?" He asked.

"No, that was just one part of my question. I may be really smart. Actually I know I have a lot of book smarts, but I have never wanted to go to college, it just never really interested me. I figure when I got out of high school that was it, I don't want to go on. So I was wondering if I do a good job helping the bad kids here and they actually respect me could I possibly have a job when I am done here? That is if I still don't want to go to college." I asked.

"It seems like you have thought a lot about the not going to college. I have to say I would like for you to go to college, but I can't force you and I won't force you. When the time comes if you think it is best for you not to go to college then yes you may have a job here. That is if you take this seriously and do a good job. There are some rules I figure I should tell you now, before you break one of them. The teachers and people that work here have as many rules as the students, which means you'll have double the responsibilities and codes to follow. You can not insult or threaten one of the students. Keep the cursing to a low, if you believe the only way someone will listen is if you swear then you can, but if you don't have to don't. You are not allowed to make deals, like you and Kim made. There is no blackmailing. This one I don't have to tell the teachers, but I figure since you are dealing with people your own age I better say something; you can not flirt or anything like that to get your way. No seducing them, or saying you like them, please I don't want to hear about that. Also I know you have made friends here; if one of them comes in you are not allowed to pick favorites. Like if there is a fight between two people I'll just use Bryce and someone you don't like. Do not go taking Bryce's side right away, because he is your boyfriend. I'll try not to send people you are good friends with to you. That would be unfair to you. Do understand everything?"

"Yeah, everything is clear, and you don't have to worry about me "seducing" anyone. I don't think that would go over too well with Bryce. And trust me I *do not* want to ruin things with him."

"I realize you care about him; I just wanted to bring the point up that you're not allowed to do any of that. I just don't want to take a chance. I do know people use their beauty to get people to do what they want. It can work too, I just don't want you to do that. It is disgraceful to you and to this school. I'm not saying I thought you were going to do that, I just want to make sure you don't. Okay?"

"I get it," I just still couldn't believe he'd think I'd do that. I know it is disgraceful, which is why I wouldn't do that. Maybe before I came here I would, but I have changed in a short period of time. I was glad I did. I mean there are something's that I miss from before I came here. For example, the freedom to leave at anytime. Actually just being able to leave. I haven't ever seen the town here or any other people, than the people that are here everyday. I missed that. Seeing the same people every single day gets kind of lame. I was heading toward the door when I decided to ask Shawn something, "Shawn?"

"Yeah, kid."

"Would there be any way someone could take me to town to get some stuff to liven up this office? I'll behave there, and if you were to go with me you could even keep an eye on me."

"How would you be able to buy anything? You don't have any money."

"Actually, my dad just gave me a check for $500. He said it was to get anything I want and there are three things that I want to get."

"And what are those three things?" Shawn asked suspiciously.

"One is some stuff for this office; two is a round trip ticket for DeDe's granddaughter to come here for her retirement party; and the third I'm not quite sure yet, but I know I want to get something for someone," I actually did know what I wanted to get. Well, not exactly, but it was for Shawn's birthday, so I couldn't go telling him.

"I guess I can take you up there now you can get the things for the office now. The other thing is going to have to wait. But you have to hurry because be have to be back in an hour and a half."

"Okay, thanks Shawn. We'll also have to stop at the bank and get my check cashed."

"Alright, just remember what I said, that we have to be quick."

"Okay, maybe we should leave then since we have to be back soon."

"Yeah, I just have to tell Kim; go wait in my jeep the passenger door should be unlocked," Shawn instructed.

"Okay," I said heading out the door to his jeep. As I was walking over there Bryce ran over to me.

"Hey baby," He greeted me.

"Hi Bryce."

"I heard from the grapevine that Shawn is going to legally be your guardian," He said and it surprised me that people have already heard about it.

"Jeez, news really travel fast around here," I commented.

"This is a small school news does really travel fast. Plus we have people here who are the best eavesdroppers, it has been their life," Bryce exclaimed.

"I mean I don't mind people finding this out, they're bond to find out sooner or later, but that is really rude. What if I was talking about my problem to my father I don't exactly want the whole student body of this school finding that out."

"Well, there are only me, you, Shawn, and Kaye that know it."

"Actually Angel knows too. Something happened that made me have to tell her," I clarified.

"Okay, well her too then. I can guarantee no one else knows about that. If anyone did we would already know it," Bryce told me which didn't make the situation any easier.

"Well, I have to go Shawn is coming he is taking me into town to get some stuff," I said and waved good bye to him and went running off. I hopped into the jeep and less than a minute later Shawn got in looking all stressed.

"You okay Shawn?" I asked.

"Yeah, I'm fine," He answered and I knew he was lying.

"You sure don't look fine."

"It's just Kim, sometimes she can really get to me. She thinks I am favoring you from everyone else."

"Well, does she know you are going to be my guardian?" I asked.

"Actually…I don't believe she does."

"It seems like everyone else does. Bryce heard it through the "grapevine". But if she doesn't know that then I guess she does make a little bit of sense saying you favor me. Maybe you should tell her and make her realize if you do act like you favor me that is why, but you don't mean to."

"You give pretty good advice, kid. You'll definitely do good at your job." We drove the rest of the way in silence. We went to the bank and then the store. "Well, here we are, Jacob's Office Supplies." The place was very small, but then it seemed like everything else in this town was small too. We walked in and Shawn seemed to know everyone in there. "You go and get what you want and I want to talk to Jacob," Shawn told me.

"Okay," I answered. I wandered around and found a nice little lamp that I thought was cute, so I had to have it. I also got some colorful post-its, a few notebooks, a bottle of whiteout, a lot of colored gel pens, and a few little things just to liven up the office a little. For example cute, little heart and butterfly shape pillows.

"You got everything you needed?" Shawn asked when I walked up to the counter.

"Yeah, I think so," I answered. He helped me put the things on the counter.

"Hang on one second. I'll have Christian ring your stuff up and Shawn come with me and I'll get you what you asked for," Jacob said. "Christian can you please ring her up?"

"Yeah sure," A tall dark haired boy answered and walked over. "Hi," He said to me.

"Hey."

"Do you go to Shawn's school?" He asked and I nodded. For some reason I felt kind of embarrassed about that. "That's cool."

"I guess, except for why I am there," I joked and he laughed.

"It will be $35.72." I got out my money and gave it to him. "So what's your name?"

"Candy," I answered.

"I'm Christian it's nice to meet you," He said shaking my hand. "Are you allowed to go on dates in that school?" He asked and I was thinking great, a guy hitting on me and I have to turn him down.

"I'm not sure, but I have a boyfriend, so even if I was allowed to I wouldn't," I told him.

"Oh does he go to that school?"

"Yeah."

"What's his name I may know him? Shawn brings a lot of the students in here and I remember almost everyone, plus some of them I'd go and hang out with."

"His name is Bryce Ashford," I answered.

"Yep, I know him, maybe sometime I'll have to visit him and ask him if he can make an exception and let you go out with me once."

"You can try, but I doubt it will work," I said to him and luckily Shawn came back out.

"You ready to go?" He asked.

"Yeah Shawn," I answered.

"Bye Candy, hopefully I'll see you around," Christian said to me.

"C-ya," Was all I said and went walking out the door to Shawn's jeep as he was saying good-bye to Jacob.

"You were quick in getting out of there," Shawn said as he got in the car.

"I was getting too tempted," I answered.

"What do you mean?"

"A cute guy was hitting on me and I almost started my old routine of charming him," I explained.

"Oh I see. I'll tell you this; Christian is a good guy. He's smart, friendly, a good all around boy, but he is a smooth talker and he usually can get his way with a girl," Shawn informed me.

"I'll tell you it didn't work on me, but there is one thing he said that I don't want to happen."

"And what is that?"

"He said he may have to come and visit Bryce, so he can see me. I may have been able to resist this time, but if I am ever alone with him again I won't be able to. I don't think I'll ever be able to change myself that much. I may be able to stop sleeping with guys unless I love them and stop doing drugs. But I honestly don't think I can stick to one guy and that is it. I love attention so much that I rather have two or three guys I can make out with, rather than just one. And that scares me, because I don't want to lose Bryce," I told Shawn.

"Well, I don't know really how I can help you there, but I will tell you a few things that may be able to help. First off I know for a fact you care about Bryce and you care about him so much that you won't let yourself hurt him. And I know that Bryce cares about you. And it isn't because of your looks or "talents" I'll say. He cares about you. He told me this one time; he was saying to me how he really likes you. He's like that girl is so amazing, she funny, smart, and beautiful...inside and out. Don't ever tell him I told you that, but he adores you. If you told him to jump he'd say how high, if you told him to go away he'd say how far, and if you told him to love you he'd say already done. Candy you two are such a great couple. Why do you think I let you and him be alone when I am not suppose to?" I shrugged my shoulders. "I swear when...or if you and Bryce ever break up. It will be a cold day in hell, pardon my language. I know that kind of love. I had it and kind of still do."

"You and Kim," I interrupted.

"How did you know?" He asked.

"Duh...the way you look at her, and the way she looks at you; it's obvious Shawn. But I can tell you that you like her more than she likes you. I think she may be a little scared to get close to you; and I am guessing it is because of what happened in your past. I know that you two must have been something before and then one of you split. I'm guessing it was you, am I correct?"

"You're amazing, you know that? You can get all that out of just the way we look at each other?" Shawn questioned.

"Shawn, I have been around guys forever, I know how they act, I know how they look at girls, and most of all I know how they feel for girls. I can almost understand them as much as girls. Besides girls can tell things by the way a guy looks at her. That is how I knew Zeke was a jerk and only wanted one thing out of me. Girls have senses like that. You put a guy and a girl together and put me in the same room as them and I can tell you exactly what they think of each other. I know that Hobie has a thing for Angel and she likes him too. They both don't know that the other one likes them though."

"What did you get out of Christian's eyes?" Shawn asked and I didn't really think about it before.

"Well, he didn't have the look that is 'I want to get in your pants', but he also didn't have the look Bryce gives me."

"I don't think anyone will give you the same look as Bryce gives you," Shawn interrupted.

"Yeah, I guess not. But I didn't mean the exact same look as Bryce does; I just mean the same loving look he gives me. The 'excited to see me look, the your special look, the you're my girl look'; you know?"

"Yeah I think I follow."

"The look in his eyes were like 'you're a pretty girl, you seem nice, and I'd like to get to know you' look. The look a normal teenage guy gives a girl he'd like to take out sometime," I explained to him.

"I don't think that is a normal teenage guy look. A normal teenage guy look is 'damn your hot, we're going out'. Trust me I know these things, I was a normal teenage guy at one point," Shawn said making me snicker. We pulled into the school and he grabbed my arm and said, "Just remember to be careful with any guy."

"I will," I answered and went running off to my office to get all my stuff together. I walked in and there was Bryce sitting on the couch. "You scared me," I said after I caught my breath of being scared.

"Well, I was a bad boy and I believe I may need some guidance," He told me with a sly smile on his face.

"Oh you need some guidance?" I questioned flirtatiously.

"Yeah," He answered getting up.

"Really? I may just be able to help." I walked over to him and we started kissing...heavy. When we were done I moved back and he said,

"That may have helped," Just then Shawn walked in.

"Hi Bryce, are you helping her get her office ready?" He asked.

"Oh yeah, I'm helping, but unfortunately I have to go. Candy, maybe I'll come back sometime for some more guidance," Bryce said and went running out of the door.

"What did he mean by that?" Shawn asked giving me a questioning look.

"I have no idea; he was probably just joking around," I answered hoping he couldn't tell that I was lying.

"Yeah, I bet," Shawn said and moved over and sat down on the couch. I didn't say anything more about that; I knew better than to.

"Do you really think I will do a good job?" I asked.

"As long as I don't send Bryce to you, yes I believe you will do a great job," he answered definitely boosting my esteem.

"Okay thanks."

"You better get to your room. It's almost time for bed," Shawn told me.

"Yeah, I am pretty tired. Good-night Shawn and thanks for taking me to the store," I said and gave him a hug.

Chapter 12

After class was over I went to my office and got ready to get down to business. There was a knock at the door about ten minutes after I got settled in.

"Yes, come in," I called.

"Hey Candy, did you have a good day?" Shawn asked walking in.

"Very good, and you?" I asked feeling very important.

"Very busy, well here is your first victim." He brought in this boy that had short dark brown hair, brown eyes; he was quite tall and thin. He was actually very good looking.

"Okay thank you Shawn," I said as he was closing the door behind him. "You can sit down there," I told the boy pointing to the couch.

"Aren't you a student here?" The boy asked.

"Actually yes I am; I'm Candy."

"Why do they have you working?" He asked with a confused look on his face.

"Shawn believes I could help. He believes maybe students will listen better to another student."

"Yeah right."

"I'll let him be the judge of that. What's your name?" I asked him.

"Don't you have a sheet on me?"

"Yeah, but I rather hear things from you rather than looking at a stupid sheet," I told him.

"Sure, I'm Antonino Mintello; Nino for short."

"That's a cool name," I commented.

"Thanks."

"So what did you do to grace my presence?"

"I'm bad."

"You're being quite vague. I don't like it when people are vague," I remarked.

"Fine; I have been giving teachers a hard time and I get in fights."

"Now was that that difficult?"

"You think I am going to tell you anything. Plus, you got a real attitude problem."

"I do not need your attitude, I got one of my own. And I don't have an attitude problem, it is suppose to be like this," I remarked and he snickered.

"Aren't you Bryce's chick?"

"I am no ones chick; I am however Bryce's girlfriend," I answered him.

"Oh, so you're also the girl that Zeke is going to get into bed, right?"

"Yeah right, maybe in Zeke's mind I will, but in reality here, not a chance," I responded. "We aren't here to talk about me though; unfortunately for you we got to talk about you."

"Great," He said sarcastically.

"Yeah it probably won't be my favorite subject either," I said to him.

"You can be really mean."

"Ain't it great. It took me long enough to be mean to people. So if you don't mind me asking how did you end up in this school?"

"My mom talked the police into letting me come here rather than having me go to the joint."

"By the joint you mean a Juvenile Detention Hall?" I asked.

"Yeah, well I was headed there for graffiti, for robbing, drinking underage, and the biggest thing…hitting a teacher."

"Oh, yeah that can definitely get you booked."

"You don't have to tell me that."

"I see in your records that your father past away when you were 16 and that's when all the trouble seemed to start. Is that the reason you started getting into trouble?"

"Is my dad dying the reason I got in trouble, is that what you're asking?"

"Yeah, I know people that when someone close to them dies they change and it usually isn't in a good way," I commented.

"Maybe he had something to do with it," He answered.

"Maybe?" I questioned.

"Okay yeah, when he died I didn't want to do work, I lost all respect for authority, I started staying away from home all night, cause it reminded me of him. If that makes any sense," He told me.

"Actually it makes perfect sense. It happens to millions of kids or teenagers or even some adults. You just have to...not forget, but just let go of the hold you have on your father. Remember all the good times you two had together and cherish them and even though you can't have any more good times you shouldn't turn all bad. I don't think your father would like that; I am guessing that he would like you to go on and live your life without getting in trouble," I explained and then realized I could give good advice.

"You're smart, you know that? I think I'll take your advice. Trust me I won't be back in here for any bad reasons, I promise you that," Nino told me.

"Well, don't do all this for me, do it for yourself."

"Thank you, and I'll c-ya around."

"Bye Nino and you're welcome," I said opening the door for him. As I was just closing the door Shawn pushed it open.

"So how did it go?" He asked.

"Very very good, he said he wasn't ever going to be back in here for bad reasons. I think I actually gave someone good advice that won't kill him."

"Wait wait, you got through to Nino Mintello on the first day?" He questioned.

"Yeah, it wasn't difficult; I just took what I knew about being bad and related it to him and told him to do the opposite. Why are you so surprised?" I asked.

"That is Zeke's best friend," He told me and I was shocked.

"Whoa...surprise comes to mind. Well, I don't understand...I got Zeke's best friend to change his ways. Zeke's best friend, right?"

"Yeah, you are good," Shawn complimented me.

"Thank you."

"Since I figured he would take you all night I didn't have anyone else scheduled to come here, so you're free to leave," Shawn said and at that moment Bryce walked in.

"What are you doing here?" I made the mistake of asking.

"Two reasons, one Nino Mintello came up to me and said I was so lucky to have a genius as a girlfriend and also I think I have been bad and need some Candy therapy," He answered and I shot him a mad look.

"Bryce," I said.

"What?"

"Don't," Was all I had to say and he got the hint to shut up because of Shawn.

"Sorry, I was just kidding. Not about the genius though," He said.

"You better have been kidding or I will be giving you some of Shawn therapy," Shawn warned him.

"I was kidding," He repeated.

"Well, you have an hour till dinner, Candy I would like you to do your homework," Shawn told me and right then and there I realized yep he is definitely my guardian.

"Alright Shawn," I said and he left. "Don't you ever do that!" I yelled and playfully slapped Bryce in the chest.

"I'm sorry I couldn't resist, plus I didn't realize Shawn was going to get mad about it. I thought he'd just take it as a joke."

"He may have taken it as a joke before he became my guardian, but not now that he is. He is like a father figure to me and he is gonna act like it. Besides you saying that is not only gonna get you in trouble, but it will also get me in trouble too."

"I'm sorry, I won't do it anymore, unless Shawn isn't around, okay?" He said and leaned in for a kiss, but I turned away.

"Nope, you have lost your kissing privileges for the rest of the day," I told him with a smile on my face.

A. M. Lahrs

"No," He said and kissed me anyway, but I didn't pull back. "You need any help with your homework?" He asked me.

"Nope, all I have is math and you know I am the genius here," I joked.

"Well, good because I do need help with math homework. Can you please help me?" He asked.

"Yeah of course." I helped Bryce for the whole hour before dinner. I also got my homework done. "So did any of that get stuck into your brain."

"I hate to say it, but yeah it did," He answered and I was completely and totally confused.

"Why do you hate to say that?" I questioned.

"Because, then you won't have to help me and I love you helping me. Let's go to dinner," He suggested taking my hand. We walked to the cafeteria and got our food.

"I think we should have a pool and whoever guesses what all this stuff is wins it," I suggested pointing at my tray and everyone laughed.

"If you start gambling, you also start community service," Shawn popped up from behind us.

"Shawn listen closely, it...was...a...JOKE!" I yelled out.

"Are you starting to get an attitude to me?" He asked.

"Do you honestly think I am going to go breaking the rules when my guardian is the owner of this place? I am not that stupid, give me some credit. Or wait is making a joke about breaking a rule another no no here?" I asked.

"Candy, bring your tray and come to my office," He ordered me.

"Fine, but I am right on this, bye guys," I said with a smile on my face and waved. We walked to his office in silence and when we walked in DeDe was sitting at her desk. "Hey DeDe, what's up?"

"Hi honey, nothing much here, but it seems like you have something going on," She said to me eyeing Shawn.

"Yeah, no kiddin'," I answered back.

"Enough chit chat, Candy," Shawn said opening the door to his room, when I sat down he slammed the door which made me jump about four feet in the air.

"Jeez, ya think you could slam it louder?"

"What is up with you today? First the thing in your office with Bryce, the attitude in the cafeteria, and now you just acting like a little snob."

"Sorry...actually no I'm not." He looked so surprised, "The thing in my office was Bryce, how was I suppose to know he was going to say that. The attitude in the cafeteria was because; you made a huge deal out of a joke I made. The joke was not making fun of anyone or hurting anyone, so I think you should have just left it at that. Now me acting like this, is just a hint to you that I shouldn't have to be in here right now. You may be my guardian, but you're not a dictator to me. Don't go telling me what I should be saying and what I shouldn't be, especially when it is a harmless joke. Also you need to understand that Bryce is my boyfriend and just because we are locked up here it doesn't me that we aren't gonna talk like we are couple and act like we are. If you honestly think we don't joke around about doing stuff that we wouldn't do or that we never kiss, then you are completely naïve and you need to get a clue Shawn," I told him getting up and walking out of his office.

"Candy!" I heard him yell, but I didn't walk back.

"I'll c-ya DeDe," I told her and waved. I walked back to the cafeteria dropped my tray in the garbage and walked out. I was so mad that I didn't want to be around people.

"Candy!" I heard someone call from behind me. I turned around and there was Nino running towards me.

"Hi Nino," I said.

"What's wrong?" He asked.

"Oh, just Shawn is pissing me off majorly; why did I agree for him to be my guardian? Oh wait, because if I didn't I would have been put up for adoption."

"Really?" He questioned.

"Yeah really."

"You want to have some fun to cheer you up?" He asked.

"What kind of fun?" I asked expecting it to be something really wrong.

"Go get your bathing suit on and I'll show you something," He ordered.

"Alright," I answered still questioning it. I went to my room and got changed. He took me to the lake and told me to wait right by the edge of it.

"Hey up here!" He yelled. He was standing on a branch of a huge weeping willow tree. All of a sudden he jumped into the water and then swam over to me.

"Whoa."

"Care to give it a try?" He asked half expecting me to say no.

"Damn right I would!" I yelled as I ran ahead.

"Hey wait up!" He called chasing after me. He showed me the easiest way to climb up the tree. We got up to the branch and jumped together.

"That was great!" I yelled as I surfaced.

"What are you two doing?" Someone yelled from over by the side of the lake.

"Oh great," I mumbled. "Hi Shawn," I called as I was swimming over to him. I knew I was going to get in trouble by the tone of his voice.

"What were you doing?" He asked me as I walked out of the water.

"Taking a little swim," I answered.

"You are not allowed to go for a little swim."

"Why not?" I asked.

"You can't go for a swim without a counselor watching you," He told me looking very disappointed.

"Why?" I asked.

"You know you're not allowed to go swimming without someone watching."

"No, I didn't. You told me there were three rules, no drugs, no violence, and no sex. I haven't broken those. Now you are telling me there are more than those rules and I get in trouble for breaking them. Like I got in trouble for leaving the school grounds looking for you and now I am guessing I will be getting in trouble for going for a swim. How was I supposed to know that I wasn't allowed to do that? Please, write down all the rules of this place, so I at least know that I am breaking a rule when I do something."

"I'm sorry, it is just I figured you would know some of the rules by just guessing. You won't get in trouble for this, but next time you want to do something ask first, so you won't get into trouble, okay?"

"Yeah sure," I answered.

"Now as for you, Nino. You know you aren't allowed to go swimming without someone; we've been over this before. You on the other hand will be punished," Shawn said.

"Yeah, I know I will be."

Chapter 13

The next few days went by pretty quick. I had a full schedule; I went to my classes, went to my office and helped people, then every few days I would practice the song for Shawn's birthday with the group. I just barely had any more than five minutes alone time with Bryce. I now know why Shawn's school worked so well; they kept you too busy to even have a chance to think about using any drugs.

It was May 21st and Shawn's birthday party was in one hour and I was so nervous. I was in my room getting ready; Kaye, May, Angel, and AJ were also there.

"I don't think I can do this," I cried out.

"Sure you can, you have been practicing and you sound great!" May said trying to encourage me.

"But when I practice there are only like ten people there, not the whole school and some of Shawn's friends," I announced.

"Just pick one person out of the crowd and picture them in their underwear," Angel said and the other girls laughed.

"Girls are you ready?" Kim asked knocking on our door.

"Come on in Kim," May called to her.

"Oh you girls looks so pretty," She complimented us.

"Thank you, Kim," We all said. We all had dresses on. Angel's dress was a pale pink with darker pink flowers on it that went to her knees. May had a long velvet burgundy color dress on. Kaye had on a long black velvet dress with black sequins on the top part. AJ had a silver silky dress that had jewels on the top that went just past her knees. I had on a baby blue dress that had different blue flower prints on it and it was ruffled at the top; it was just a little bit above my knees.

"Okay, come on girls we have to go to the cafeteria. Shawn's friends should be bringing him back soon," Kim informed us. When we got there the whole school was there. The Spruce Falls were to get on stage. Shawn came less than five minutes later. We turned off the lights and waited for him to open the door. He walked in with his friends and we all yelled,

"Surprise, Happy Birthday Shawn!" At that time I was suppose to go up to the microphone and say a little speech and then sing the song.

"Hi Shawn. Happy Birthday! All of us want to thank you in our own special way for our own reasons. You helped us all with anything and everything. You encourage us, teach us, listen to us, and show us there is a meaning for life. I don't know about everyone else, but I know you have been my hero. When I thought there was no good in this world or in me you showed me other wise. You saved my heart and my life. You told me that you believed in me and told me that I had a place in this world. When everything in my life seemed to be spinning you made them stop and pointed me in the right direction. This is for you from all of us in the Spruce Falls group," I said and started singing *Wind Beneath My Wings*. At the chorus the group joined in. We sounded like a choir of angels; we hit every note perfectly and sounded great together. When we were done I came back up to the microphone and added; "You truly are our guardian angel and our wind beneath our wings. Happy Birthday Shawn; we all love you." I looked down at him and he was crying.

I jumped off the stage with the gift that DeDe took me out to get one day.

"You were amazing," He complimented me in tears. "And you said you couldn't sing in front of people," He added.

"Thank you Shawn; I got you a gift," I told him handing a wrapped box. He opened it up and he wrapped me in his arms tightly. I had gotten him a plaque that engraved on it said:

'A father is a watcher; a caring soul.
He guides you when you're lost and shows you where to go.
He's my tissue when I cry, my sunshine when it pours.
And when I am feeling closed in, he shows me the open doors.
Happy Birthday, Shawn.
The greatest father I have ever known.
Love Candy'

"Candy, this is the greatest gift I could have ever gotten; thank you," He spoke with tears running down his face as he hugged me.

"I'm glad you like it; I had it made specially. I wrote down the poem and they engraved it for me."

"You made that poem?" He questioned.

"Yeah, DeDe helped me with some of it, but I mostly did it," I replied.

"I'm so thankful and honored to have you as my daughter," He said and I was speechless when I could speak I did.

"Shawn you don't know how much that means to hear that from you. No one has every said they were honored to have me in anyway, whether it was as a friend, a lover, or a member of the family. Hearing it come out of you means the world and more to me. Shawn, I am also honored to have you as my father; there is no one I would rather have as my father. I mean that with all my heart and soul." I wrapped my arms around him and gave him a great bear hug and he returned it with a bear hug and lifted me into the air. I was so happy; I have never been this happy in all my life. This has been the best day of my life and I wouldn't give it up for anything and everything in this world.

After the party was over Shawn called me to his office. I walked in there and he was sitting at his desk smiling.

"Hey what's up?" I said as I took a seat on the couch.

"I want to say thank you for everything."

275

"What do you mean?" I questioned.

"Well, that plaque is amazing; I am going to be hanging it up on the wall here. Also for getting up in front of all those people and showing them and me your beautiful talents. Most importantly I want to thank you for agreeing for me to adopt you. You are an amazing little or I should say young lady and I am honored and pleased to call you family."

"Shawn, I should be the one thanking you. You helped me so much."

"Well, let's just put it like this; we are both very thankful."

"I like that idea," I replied.

"As you know the year is almost over. Every summer the students get off for a week to see their family and then they spend the rest of the summer here. It turns into camp for them all; we don't have any classes here. We just do some fun stuff. I was wondering if for that week that everyone goes home, if you'd like to come home with me? I mean I know you have never been to my house and I don't know if you usually do something else or what you'd like to do this summer, but if there isn't anything else you have to do would you like to come to my house?" He asked and I knew I couldn't say no. I didn't have any reason to say no.

"I'd love to Shawn," I accepted.

"Great! You better get to bed. Oh, and Candy we have a court date in a week for the adoption."

"That's great! Is my mom, dad, and Clint going to be there?" I asked.

"Well, your mother and father definitely will be there, but Clint I'm not sure of. He could, I wouldn't find it wise for him to be there, but it is possible that he will," Shawn exclaimed.

"Well, I can't wait till I won't be a Walkinson anymore. Will I have to keep my last name or will I have yours?" I asked.

"It's up to you."

"Well, I'd be honored to have your name," I said and walked out of his office.

Chapter 14

When Shawn and I had to go to the courtroom I was ready for it. I was so happy that I was going to officially be in Shawn's family. I had to get dressed up that day. I was wearing a velvet black dress that went up to my knees. I walked out of my room to wait for Shawn.

"Hi, Candy; are you ready to go?" Shawn was wearing black dress pants and a forest green silky dress shirt.

"Now, don't you look handsome," I complimented him.

"Well, thank you." We got in his jeep and we both were silent on the ride there. I'm not sure exactly what Shawn was thinking about, but I was guessing that he was thinking the same thing as I was; about how much both our lives are going to change after today. Him having to take care of a daughter and me having just a father, when I was use to just the opposite. We pulled into the parking lot and I saw my mom's car already there and I was pretty sure my dad's pickup was there too. I walked into the building with Shawn's arm around my shoulders. Which made me feel safe. We walked to where Shawn was told to go, but before we went into the room Shawn stopped me.

"You are okay with all of this, right?"

"Yeah, definitely," I answered.

"You're not having any second thoughts?" He questioned.

"No, Shawn; I am totally and completely sure about all this," I assured him.

"Good," He said and led me into the room. I saw seated at one side of the table my father and at the other side was my mother and...Clint.

"Why does he have to be here?" I whispered to Shawn, but he just shrugged. I could have talked regularly, because my parents were fighting and screaming at each other. And I figured they would be like this.

"He's probably trying to get to you Candy, but don't let him." When Clint saw me he went to get up, but my mother stopped him.

"Candace," My mother said coldly.

"Mrs. Walkinson," I responded in the same tone. "Hi dad," I said and went to hug my dad.

"I figured you'd be mad at me," He remarked.

"No, I understand and I think it is for the best," I replied.

"Well, I'm glad."

"Hi Candy," Clint said and it was differently than he has ever talked to me. His tone wasn't cold and didn't make a shiver go up my spine; it was actually just the opposite. I then realized why; he was hoping I would forget about all the stuff he has done. Well, he had another thing coming to him. I refused to say hi back to him.

"Come on kid, let's take a seat," Shawn said and led me to the end of the table. A few minutes later the judge came in.

"Good morning everyone," She greeted us.

"Morning," We all said in unison.

"I am Judge Bremen. So we are here today to have Miss Candace Walkinson adopted to Mr. Shawn Jensen," She said looking through a folder. "Candace, right?" She questioned pointing at me.

"Yes, Ma'am," I answered politely.

"How do you feel about this?" She asked me.

"I'm happy with it. Shawn is great; he has showed me the love a family should give each other and I want to continue that," I answered truthfully.

"Mr. Jensen what is your occupation?"

"I am the owner and advisor of the school Long Ridge."

"Does Candace attend that school?" She asked.

"Yes she does."

"Does she live on the campus?"

"Yes, all the students do, in fact."

"What kind of a school is this?" She questioned.

"It is a high school for troubled teens. We help teenagers, who have done things from drugs to stealing to fighting to having eating disorders," He answered.

"Okay, well that's a very generous thing of you to do. To help kids whom have problems."

"It's a great job; I meet some exceptional young men and women. Candace here is probably one of the most amazing students I have ever had."

"At the times when she won't be living at the school do you have a place for her? Do you have a room that can be hers alone?" She asked.

"Yes, my house has three extra rooms, so if she ever wants a friend to stay over for a week or so. I have plenty of room for her."

She asked many more questions to Shawn, my parents, and me. By the end of the meeting my hands were tired from signing millions of papers and Shawn was granted full custody of me and we got to leave as a family. We just had to see someone every two months for the next two years, just to make sure we are doing okay together. When we got in the car I mentioned this to Shawn,

"Do you realize we walked in there with a student, teacher relationship and we have just walked out of there as a family?"

"It's a great feeling, huh?"

"Absolutely!" I cried out.

"So would you like to go out for lunch with me...daughter?" He asked smiling.

"I'd love to...father," I answered and we both laughed together. "It's okay that I still call you Shawn, right?" I questioned when we finished laughing.

"I wouldn't expect you to call me dad cause I'm not exactly that and I wouldn't let you call me Mr. Jenson. You didn't when we weren't family and I certainly wouldn't let you know that we are. So there isn't really anything else you can call me. Or at least nothing that else that is appropriate."

"Okay, I just wanted to make sure you didn't expect me to call you dad all the time. As much as I wish you were my real father you're not and it'd feel weird calling you that," I informed him.

"Yeah I get it." We went out for lunch as our first meal as a family, but then that special moment had to end and we had to drive back to the school. "We're home," Shawn announced as he pulled into the school.

"Or at least as close as home as I'll ever get," I said as I got out of the jeep. I turned back to Shawn and I saw in his eyes that my comment stung him. "I'm sorry, I didn't mean it like that," I quickly apologized.

"No...don't be sorry, you're right, this isn't your home or the type of home you should have, but it's the best I can give you now. I swear though somehow I will change it. I don't know when or how, but I will. I promise," He swore.

"Shawn, don't worry about it. I love it here as if it was my home. I just think that I have many brothers and sisters to live with me.

Some of which I don't really like, but hey you
know the saying 'there's a rotten egg in every
family', well here we go," I joked. I got a
smile out of him, which made me feel better
about that. "I got to go; I told Bryce I would
go and see him when we got back. I'll c-ya
Shawn," I told him gave him a hug and went
jogging off to find Bryce. I went to his room
and he wasn't there. I saw Harrison not too far
away. I went running over to him.

"Hi, Candy. How did it go today in court?"
He said as he saw me running over to him.

"It went good," I answered.

"Well, that's good, so what's up? Wait let
me guess, you're looking for Bryce."

"Right, do you happen to know where he
is?" I asked.

"I am guessing at the basketball court;
there's a game going on there and you know
Bryce. If there's a game he's there," Harrison
joked.

"Yeah, thanks a bunch. I'll see you later," I
said and walked off. Just as Harrison said
Bryce was playing basketball with a lot of
other guys, including Hobie, Jay, and Jackson.
I walked over there and sat down on the grass.
He saw me and waved to me and I naturally

waved back. Not long after Angel came wandering over and sat down next to me.

"Hi, Angel," I said as she was sitting down.

"Hi, how did the court thing go?" She politely asked.

"It went good, Shawn is officially my legal guardian."

"That's great."

"Yeah it is, so how have you been doing?"

"I'm good," She answered.

"It's amazing that we share a room, yet we barely ever get to actually talk."

"I know and I wish it wasn't like that. I enjoy talking to you; you have done so much for me. You stood up for me when you first came, you helped me with the Zeke incident and also ever since you have been around I have been more outgoing."

"Well, I am glad I have helped; even if I didn't realize I was helping you, but we should really try and make time for us to talk."

"Do you realize that this year is almost over? In just three weeks May, Jay, Jackson and Harrison will be graduating from here," She informed me.

"I didn't know it was that close; it's going to be weird without May being here with us."

"I know I'm really going to miss her," Angel said looking down at the grass.

"Is something wrong Angel?" I asked.

"Yeah, but I don't really want to talk about it with all these people around," She told me.

"Well, then let's go take a walk," I told her standing up. We started walking to the lake. "So what's up girl?" I asked.

"Well, in two weeks everyone's parents come here and I really don't want my mom to come."

"Yeah, I remember you saying how you don't get along with your mom so much."

"It's not that we fight, it's just she makes me feel like I'm not right."

"Right?" I questioned.

"As if I'm not good enough for her, you know what I mean?" She asked.

"Yeah I understand completely; I use to think that I wasn't good enough for people. Then I started to think the other way around and jeez that was even worse," I joked and she smiled.

"She just always makes me feel so low," She told me as her smile faded.

"Don't worry so much about it. Just remember the only person who can make you inferior is yourself. People can try to make you feel low, but you never will be unless you start believing them, so hint, hint don't believe them," I explained to her and she just smiled back.

"Thanks," She said.

"Not a problem. Are all the parents coming?" I asked.

"Yeah, well, except the parents who aren't having anything to do with their kids."

"Will Bryce's parents be coming?" I asked.

"I am guessing his father will, why?" She asked.

"I wonder if he knows about me at all, I mean I am most likely going to be meeting him."

"I'm sure that he does know about you. I mean Bryce can't keep his mouth shut about you. I swear the guys like you a lot, but they are going to get sick of hearing about you. I mean one time Bryce and I were working together and we didn't get any work done. He was only talking about how much fun you were, how pretty you were, how amazing you are. He seriously won't ever keep his mouth shut about you. So I am sure that if he has talked to his father you were brought up in their conversation many of times," Angel told me making me laugh.

"Well, I hope he is as fond of me as Bryce is," I replied.

"I don't think he couldn't be. I mean is there anyone who seriously does not like you here?"

"Not too my knowledge, but I mean there probably are."

"I doubt it; the only people who could hate you are people who are jealous of you. I mean you have a great personality, you are nice to people, unless they piss you off, you never argue with people, and you are great when it comes to helping people. You are an all around nice, great, considerate person," She complimented me.

"Well, thank you and if I get all teary eyed right now I'm coming after you," I kidded. "I got to go back and see if Bryce is done with his game," I told her and went running off. I went back to the basketball court and Bryce was just finishing up the game. He walked over to me and kissed me on the cheek.

"Hey girly, where'd you just go?" He asked me.

"I went to talk to Angel," I answered simply.

"Let's take a walk," He said putting his arm over my shoulders. I started to realize the only thing we ever do is take walks. I also noticed how boring it gets, but it's not Bryce's fault. Shawn wouldn't ever let us go out anywhere.

"Okay."

"So how did court go?" He questioned.

"Great, Shawn is now my legal guardian."

"Was your family there?" He asked and I knew where he was going.

"Yes Bryce, Clint was there."

"Did you..."

"No, we didn't talk. All he said was hi and it was emotionless. I figured he was trying to make me forget what happened and I didn't. My mother didn't pester me on dropping the charges. Clint didn't mention anything either. He didn't even give me a mean look or a dirty look or a look that scared me. He was technically mature about it all and so was I. Is that everything you wanted to know?"

"Yep that's about it," He replied.

"Can I ask you something?" I said as I stopped.

"Yeah, of course."

289

"Have you talked to your father recently?"

"Umm…about a week or two ago, why?"

"Did you happen to tell him about me?"

"Yeah, do you mind?"

"No, I was just wondering."

"Why?" He questioned.

"Because Angel told me in a few weeks that the parents will be coming and I just wanted to know if he knew about me."

"He does know about you. He is going to be coming and he is looking forward to meeting you. He wants to meet the girl that has a huge effect on my acting, and that has prevented me from getting into trouble. He thinks you sound perfect and of course you are. He also said that he wants you to come out to dinner with us the first night he comes. Did I cover it all?"

"Yeah."

"See you're not the only one that can answer all the questions before they were asked."

"Yep. Have I really had an effect on you?" I asked.

"Yes you have. My dad was use to getting a call from Shawn every week saying I have been acting up and now it has stopped."

"Cool. Do you think your father will like me?"

"How could he not. You are sweet, smart, funny, kind, considerate, a little cutie, plus you're a great kisser," He complimented me and then kissed me.

"I don't think your father is going to be very concerned on how I kiss."

Chapter 15

The day that the parents came to visit came up quicker than I expected. I got dressed up because Shawn asked me if I could give a group of parents the tour before dinner. I walked to where I was suppose to meet them all and they seemed to be all there.

"Hello and welcome to Long Ridge everyone. I'm Candy Wa...Jenson," I said correcting myself. "I'll be giving you the fifty cent tour," I said and started on the way. We walked in the Main Lodge first. "Here is the Main Lodge. The students come here on their free time. We play games in here, do homework, or just hang out. Sometimes some classes are held in here." We were walking to the recreational area when one of the parents walked over next to me.

"Candy, right?" She asked.

"That'd be me."

"Do you know my daughter Angela?" She asked.

"Yes I do, we actually are in the same room," I answered.

"How is she doing here?" She asked.

"Angel is very well. She's nice and keeps everyone happy by her optimism. She's a great friend and really listens to people," I answered.

"Would you say she's gained weight?"

"Not since I came here. I think she has a perfect body. She's very pretty." I knew with that question why Angel wasn't too fond of her mom.

"I'm just afraid she has gained weight and has gotten fat."

"Well, I mean it is normal for a teenager to gain weight, and just because a person does gain weight doesn't mean she's fat. It means that you're doing what is normal for your body."

"What do you know? You can probably eat whatever you want and never gain a pound."

"That's not true, but if Angel gaining weight is the thing your worried most about you should really think again," I told her and continued on with the tour. After it was over I took them all back to the cafeteria. The parents were going to sit with their kids there. I was suppose to meet Bryce and his father in the Main Lodge and then we were going out to dinner together. I walked into the lodge and Bryce was sitting on the couch alone.

"Hi, Bryce," I said as I kissed his cheek and sat down next to him.

"Hey sweetie," He responded cheerfully.

"Where's your dad?" I asked.

"He went to talk to Shawn for a bit to see where he can and can't take us. He says he has a surprise for us after we eat and he wants to make sure it is okay with Shawn."

"I wonder what it is," I told him.

"Me too, but we'll find out pretty soon, he just walked through the door." I turned around and this handsome man was walking over to us. He looked in his late 30s and he looked so much like Bryce.

"I'm back," He said to Bryce, "And this must be your famous girlfriend," He said shaking my hand.

"Dad, this is Candy, Candy my father," Bryce introduced us.

"It's nice to meet you Candy, now I know why my son is so smitten with you," He complimented me.

"Thank you, Mr. Ashford; now I know where Bryce gets his good looks."

"You're a sweetie too."

"That she is," Bryce responded putting his arm around my waist.

"Thank you both," I said. I wasn't as nervous as I thought I'd be. I always was good with parents...that is when I was sober.

"So what are we going to do, dad?" Bryce asked.

"Well, we are first going to go out to dinner. Shawn told me about this nice diner. Then I have a surprise for you two; you'll find out what that is at dinner." We drove in Mr. Ashford's new Mercedes. I then realized that Bryce's family was quite rich. We walked into the diner and Bryce pulled out the chair for me. I never realized that he was that much of a gentlemen.

"Thank you Mr. Ashford for bringing me along with you," I said to him.

"Oh, it's my pleasure. If my son loves you this much then you're a part of this family too," He replied and I felt like crying. Under the table Bryce reached over and took my hand in his. Our food came and gone; we talked a lot. I got to hear things about Bryce when he was younger. That is before he starting to use drugs. I heard about his younger brother who unfortunately had school and couldn't come.

After we were done talking and eating it was time for Mr. Ashford to announce his surprise for us.

"So dad what's the surprise?" Bryce asked. He was like a little boy on Christmas morning; that's how anxious he looked.

"Well, I was guessing that you guys can't really go anywhere, so I asked Shawn if it was okay if I dropped you off at the Movie Theater. You two can have a real date alone. I will pick you up at the Movie Theater. I am doing this one thing without Shawn's permission. I will pick you up an hour after the movies; you two can wander around. Or you can go out for ice cream, but if I do find out you did anything wrong I will deny letting you two go and I'll tell Shawn you ran away from me. And I bet Shawn will be a whole lot tougher on you than me. That is my only rule and I do expect you to follow it." Bryce and I sat there staring at each other. I can almost guarantee that we were thinking the same thing. Three hours alone, we have never ever had that.

"Dad, you really and truly are the best," Bryce burst out.

"Mr. Ashford thank you so...so...so much. This is one of the nicest things anyone has ever done."

"You both are very welcome, but remember what I said." Mr. Ashford drove us to the Movie Theaters. He dropped us off and told us he'd be back in three and a half-hours. He gave Bryce $50 to do whatever we wanted...well to an extent. We walked into the theater.

"So what movie should we see?" He asked.

"I don't really know, since we haven't exactly seen any previews. You can pick," I told him.

"Alright," He replied. He picked a movie that he thought we would enjoy. We paid for the tickets and walked in. We sat down and saw a really good movie and it was our real first date. After the movie was over we went out for ice cream. I felt as if I was a *normal* girl, with a *normal* life, out with my *normal* boyfriend, on a *normal* date.

"My dad said to me earlier that during the week we have with our families in the summer that you are welcome to come," Bryce told me as we sat down at a table in the ice cream place.   "That is if Shawn says it's okay," He quickly added.

"I'd love to, that is if Shawn agrees, but I'm sure he will."

"I love you," Bryce said leaning across the table and kissing me softly on the lips.

"I love you too," I replied after he pulled away.

"Do you know how much I truly care about you?" He questioned.

"I can guess it's the same as I care about you," I responded.   Bryce looked across the street.

"You know what?   I'll be right back," He told me as he got up from the table.

"Where are you going?" I asked.

"It's a surprise.   I'll be right back," He answered and went running off across the street.   As I was waiting there I heard a familiar voice that I couldn't figure out who it was that said hi to me.   I turned around and Christian, the guy from the store was standing there.

"Hi Christian how are you?" I asked.

"I'm very well.   How are you?"

"I'm good, great in fact."

"What are you doing here?" He questioned.

"Well, Bryce and I are out on a date," I answered and Christian was looking all around.

"I don't see him," He commented.

"Well, he went to get something. He said it was a surprise."

"Bryce isn't too wise to keep you—a very pretty girl—out on her lonesome. Strange guys may pick you up," He remarked flirtatiously.

"I can take care of myself," I assured him.

"Would you like me to keep you company while you wait for him to return."

"No, I'll be fine, but thanks anyway."

"Oh come on," He pleaded.

"No really it's all right, beside there's Bryce," I told him as I got up. "I'll see you." I went running off quite relieved. I ran to Bryce and he had both his hands behind his back.

"Who was that?" He asked.

"Christian, he works at this one store," I replied.

"Oh him."

"What do you have?" I questioned.

"I got you this," He said as he pulled a teddy bear holding a single red rose. I jumped into his arms and kissed him. "I'll take that as you like it."

"I love it Bryce." I kissed him once again, but it was more passionate. As we were kissing we heard a car beep. It was Mr. Ashford.

"I didn't realize it was this late; I wish it didn't have to end," Bryce whispered to me.

"Me either." The car pulled up next to us and we got in.

"Did you two have fun?" Mr. Ashford asked.

"Yes, thank you Mr. Ashford."

"Yeah, thanks dad."

"You're welcome. I'm glad you had fun, but now we have to get back. I have to get going too.

"You're leaving?" Bryce questioned.

"Yeah, I would love to stay longer, but I have get to work tomorrow night." Mr. Ashford drove us back to the school; Bryce and I thanked him again. I decided it best to leave Bryce and his father alone to say goodbye. I said goodbye to Mr. Ashford and goodnight to Bryce and went off. I was running to my cabin when I heard Shawn's voice. I turned around to his office and walked over to there. The door was slightly open, so I peaked in. Shawn was sitting down and he was talking on the phone.

"Is that so? I figured it be awhile till he broke," I heard Shawn say. "Well, I'll tell her tomorrow; she'll be so relieved," He told the person and hung the phone up. I had a gut feeling he was talking about me, so I knocked on the door.

"Come in," He called. I pushed opened his heavy door and walked into the room. The lamp on his desk was the only thing lighting the room.

"I just wanted to tell you that Bryce and I are back."

"Okay, Candy I have some great news," He announced as he was standing up.

"What is it?" I asked.

"You won't have to go to court because of Clint," He replied and I was confused.

"Why not?" I questioned.

"He confessed to your mother and told the police that all you said was true. He has two-four years in jail," Shawn answered and I was stunned. I couldn't move, I couldn't even think. I stood there dumbfounded. I didn't know whether I was more surprised or relieved.

"He confessed?" I questioned still not sure I heard Shawn right.

"He confessed; he told your mother that he was sorry and he told her to tell you that he apologizes. Whether or not he was serious about it isn't my call."

"It's over," I said out loud. "It's over," I repeated.

"Yeah, it's over kid," Shawn said and hugged me. "Also your mother is coming tomorrow."

"Why?" I asked surprised.

"I'm not sure, but I think she wants to apologize."

"Well, she has plenty to. Do you think she wants me back?" I questioned.

"I'm not sure, you'll have to wait till tomorrow." I walked out of Shawn's office and went to my cabin. I just grabbed the doorknob, but stopped to think for a bit and then went in.

Chapter 16

I was woken up to the sound of a blow dryer. I opened my eyes slowly and I saw AJ in the bathroom drying her hair. No one else was a round; I figured since it was Sunday they'd be spending the only free time they really had, having fun. AJ saw that I was awake and walked out of the bathroom.

"Morning," I said still groggy.

"I woke you didn't I?"

"It was the blow dryer, not you."

"I'm sorry," She apologized.

"It's okay. What time is it?" I asked.

"8:30."

"Why didn't anyone wake me up?" I questioned.

"Shawn came in and told us not to wake you up, he said he'd come to get you." I was really confused by what she told me. Shawn never let anyone sleep in, unless they were sick and he knew I wasn't.

"Do you know why he did that?"

"Nope," She responded. "I got to go, I'll talk to you later." She pranced out the door seeming happy. I figured the cause was a guy.

303

I decided I'd ask her later. I got out of bed and got changed, to head to Shawn's office.

I reached the main lodge when I saw my mother's car there. Now I really was wondering why Shawn didn't wake me. I walked to Shawn's office, but DeDe said he wasn't in. She told me that he left with some lady, I figured it was my mother. I went out to find them and I literally ran into Kim.

"Hi Candy," She greeted me.

"Hi Kim, do you know where Shawn is?" I questioned.

"I just saw him in the lodge, with a some student's mother," She answered.

"Yeah mine, well thanks Kim," I said and rushed off. I walked into the main lodge and there was Shawn sitting with my mother on the couch. I noticed Shawn wasn't looking too happy, he actually looked hurt and scared. When he saw me he wiped that look off of his face. He said something to my mother and they rose and walked to me.

"Let's go to my office," Shawn said quietly as he put his hand on my shoulder. The three of us walked to his office. When we reached the office it started to rain and it seemed right for this occasion. We sat down without saying a word, I didn't want to start the conversation, nor did I know how to.

"How have you been?" My mother said starting the conversation.

"I've had my good and bad days."

"Shawn, can you please leave us for a moment?" She asked.

"I'll be right outside if you need anything," He whispered to me and I nodded.

"Candy, I don't really know what to say to you, but I'm sorry." She put her hand over mine. "I know what I did was wrong and the first night I found out that Clint truly did all that stuff to you I cried my eyes out. I don't know how you're going to react to this next thing I say, but I want you as my daughter again." I was stunned. Before this I didn't talk to her at all. "Please talk to me," She pleaded.

"What do you want me to say?" I asked.

"I want you to say that you'll give me another chance as your mother. I heard that you've been doing great, so I would like to take you home and put this all behind us."

"What?" I questioned.

"I want you to come home and I want us to be a family again."

"You betrayed me, you disowned me, and now you want me to come back with you? I don't even know what to call you; I can't even call you Mother."

"You think I betrayed you?" She questioned.

"You believed someone who was married in, before you would believe me-your flesh and blood. Yes, I understand I made mistakes in my life, I understand I hurt you, but you did the worst. You didn't want me in your life anymore. Would it be that whenever it's convenient for you you'll be my mother? I'm sorry, but I can't go back. I'm one not ready to go out into the world and all the problems I had, two my family, my true family is here. Shawn believed in me when no one else did; Shawn kept me from being an orphan; Shawn was my family when I didn't have one; Shawn was the father I've never had; Shawn is not only my family, but he is also my teacher, my mentor, and my guardian. I can and will not leave this life. I don't want to be a daughter of someone who won't even try and believe me. I'm sorry, Mrs. Walkinson, but I don't think we should even talk anymore. Shawn is my family now not you and you're the one that made that decision," I said and got up and walked out the door. I walked out of the office and Shawn was no where to be seen, either was anyone else. It looked like a ghost town. I went wandering around to find Shawn. The rain was dripping down my face and my hair was all wet when I found Shawn. He was at the basketball courts, shooting hoops.

"Shawn," I said but he didn't hear me. "Shawn!" He stopped and looked up to me, he had the rain dripping down his face and he looked at me so sad. He walked over to me slowly. "Did she tell you what she was going to ask me?" I questioned.

"Yes she did, did she tell you?"

"Yes."

"Did you have an answer for her?" He questioned.

"Yeah I did. Shawn you have helped me more than any person I know and you've cared for me and you've taught me many things."

"But I know she's family, you have to go with her."

"She may be blood, but you are the true family. I'm staying with you," I said to him over the rain.

"You're staying?" He questioned.

"I'm not going anywhere," I said and he wrapped his arms around me and gave me the hardest hug ever. "Shawn you are my family from now, until forever. Besides I plan on graduating from here, not from some normal high school. They are so highly over rated," I joked as he pulled away.

Chapter 17

The next few days I did what I told Shawn I was planning on doing. I wanted to give DeDe a good bye party and have her granddaughter sent out here. I tracked down the famous model Emma Drake and gave her a call. She said that she'd be here for the day of the party.

The day of her retirement party came and I was so excited. She had no idea about it. All of the students helped me out with the decorations and the food and the cake. Shawn said that he would take her out for dinner and then bring her back here.

"Okay they're coming," Bryce called out. We had all the lights out. When she walked in we all screamed surprise. She had tears in her eyes. I don't think she realized all these people cared about her. I got up on stage to make the announcement of her granddaughter being here.

"DeDe I didn't really know what I should give you. I didn't really know what you would like. So I got you the only thing I knew you wanted. I got some money and a plane ticket. Here is your granddaughter Emma." Emma walked out and she was truly beautiful, she had long blond hair and blue eyes like me. She was much taller than I was, considering she was a model. I saw tears streaming down DeDe's face. "DeDe, we all love you. Thank you for the talks and the advice and the kindness you have showed me." I got off the stage and showed Emma to her grandmother. They acted as if there hasn't been any time apart between them. Seeing them act that way made me sad, I have never had a grandparent and I wish I did. I went outside and sat down on the steps.

"You know you truly are amazing," Bryce said from behind me.

"No, I'm not. I just wanted to do something special for her. I knew she wanted to see her granddaughter more than anything."

"Well, I think and know that you are the most amazing person I know," He said as he sat down next to me.

"Thank you." We were sitting there for awhile. Bryce had his arms over my shoulders and I was leaning my head down against his shoulder. We didn't even talk while sitting there.

"Candy," DeDe said from behind me. I got up off of the steps and faced her. She had a shimmer in her eyes; she looked so happy to have Emma back. "Candy, I want to thank you so much. No one could have given me a greater gift. You are a very special girl and with the kindness you have, you'll go far. I loved you as if you were a granddaughter. I will truly miss the talks we have. Thank you again and again for Emma."

"It was no problem; I was so glad to do it. You gave up your time to talk to me, so I owed you," I told her and gave her a hug. I knew today was her last day I probably would never see her again. I knew I would always remember DeDe and how nice and kind she was to me.

Chapter 18

Graduation Day came quicker than anyone anticipated. All of the last years here were discussing what they were going to do after they left. It was interesting to me to see who was going to be going to college and where. I learned most of the students were going to take a year off to straighten things out and see if

311

they can handle the pressure of college. May was one of those, waiting a year. She really wanted to go straight to college, but she was afraid that she would mess it up and go back to old routine. I respected her for her decision. Hearing everyone talk about college made me start to think. I was unsure if I'd even want to go to college. As I was sitting in my seat while waiting for the ceremony to start I thinking about working here with Shawn or even traveling around. Bryce ran in and sat down next to me, putting his arm over my shoulder.

"Why are you so late?" I asked.

"I was asking Shawn about you coming to my house for the week."

"And?"

"He said it was fine as long as my dad would be there the whole time, which he is."

"It's going to be so much fun."

"Of course it will." The ceremony came and went. Both Bryce and I were bored through out the whole thing. That was, until May, Jackson, Harrison, and Jay were called up. All of the Spruce Falls cheered for them. I don't know about everyone else, but I was proud of all of them. I couldn't wait until

Shawn was calling my name and I walked across the stage.

I knew this was the last day I would walk into my room and see May sitting on the bed. I also knew I wouldn't be able to join Jackson, Jay, and Harrison playing football. I was going to miss them all, but still I couldn't wait until it was me up there. I could even see myself walking up there in my cap and gown, but that will be another chapter of my life as Candy Jenson.

Printed in the United States
733200001B